Silver
Bells

Silver Bells

A HOLIDAY TALE

Luanne Rice

BANTAM BOOKS

SILVER BELLS
A Bantam Book / November 2004

Published by Bantam Dell
A Division of Random House, Inc.
New York, New York

Book design by Virginia Norey

Library of Congress Cataloging in Publication Data

Rice, Luanne.
Silver bells / Luanne Rice.
p. cm.
ISBN: 0-553-80411-1
I: Christmas tree industry—Fiction. II: Runaway teenagers—Fiction.
III: Widowers—Fiction. IV: Widows—Fiction.
V: New York (N.Y.)—Fiction.

PS3568.I289 S55 2004
813/.54 22—2004056634

Manufactured in the United States of America
Published simultaneously in Canada

BVG   10 9 8 7 6 5 4 3 2 1

To Brother Luke Armour

ACKNOWLEDGMENTS

With love and appreciation to Audrey and Robert Loggia.

I am grateful to E.J. McAdams, director of New York City Audubon and former Urban Park Ranger, for introducing me to the owls in Central Park and the people who treasure them.

Thank you, with love, Karen Ziemba.

For all their support, I am grateful to Juan Figueroa, Anthony Lopez, Raul Salazar, Sixto Cruz, Jerry de Jesus, and Emil Estrada.

With admiration for Mia Onorato and the BDG for their never-ending quest for all sorts of very important things.

Love to Cirillo: bandmate, photographer extraordinaire, and excellent movie date.

All my love and thanks to Irwyn Applebaum, Nita Taublib, Tracy Devine, Kerri Buckley, Barb Burg, Susan Corcoran, Betsy Hulsebosch, Carolyn Schwartz, Cynthia Lasky, Jim Plumeri, Anna Forgione, Virginia Norey, and everyone at Bantam Books.

Much gratitude to Robert G. Steele for the beautiful book jackets.

Susan, Mowgli, and Sugar Ray know the whole truth, and I'm forever grateful.

Maggie, May, and Maisie keep watch over Chelsea, and each other, and me . . .

I am so appreciative to everyone who teaches me to look past the world we can see with our eyes, in search of the things we can see with our hearts . . . especially Leslie and the memory of Father William "Rip" Collins, C.Ss.R.

Silver
Bells

All summer long the trees had grown tall and full, roots deep in the rich island soil, branches yearning toward the golden sun. The salt wind had blown in from the east, gilding the pine needles silver. Everyone knew that the best Christmas trees came from the north, with the best of all coming from Nova Scotia, where the stars hung low in the sky. It was said that starlight lodged in the branches, the northern lights charged the needles with magic. Nova Scotia trees were made hardy by the sea and luminous by the stars.

On Cape Breton's Pleasant Bay, in the remote north of Nova Scotia, was a tree farm owned by Christopher Byrne. His family had immigrated to Canada from Ireland when he was a child; they'd answered an ad to work on a Christmas tree farm. It was brutally hard work, and they were very poor, and Christy remembered going to sleep with a gnawing hunger in his belly.

By the time he was twelve, he was six feet tall, growing too fast for the family to afford—and his mother had often sacrificed her own food so her oldest child would have enough to eat. He'd need it to withstand the elements. For the north wind would roar, and Arctic snows would fly, and summer heat would blaze into flash fires, and Christy would work through it all. His mother would ring the dinner bell, to call them home from the field. He loved that sound, for no matter how little they had, his mother would do her best to make sure Christy had more than enough love and almost enough food.

His hunger had made Christy Byrne a fierce worker, and it had given him a wicked drive for success. He saved every penny he made, buying land of his own, using the skills and instincts he'd learned from his father to plant his trees and survive the brutal elements. His mother's love and generosity had made Christy a fine man, and that had made him a good father. He *knew* he was a good father. It couldn't be in doubt; he had a fire in his heart for his children. So that was why this year, cutting the trees on the mountainside in preparation for going south to sell them, he felt such a storm of hope and confusion.

Every year on the first day of December, Christy drove south to New York City. Hordes of tree salespeople would descend upon the glittering island of Manhattan, from the flatlands of Winnipeg, the snowy forests north of Toronto and east of Quebec, the green woodlands of Vermont and Maine, the lakes of Wisconsin, the lonely peninsulas of Michigan. Their trees would

be cut and tied, hauled by flatbed trucks over the brilliant garland bridges spanning the East and Hudson Rivers, offloaded on
street corners from Little Italy to Gramercy Park, from Tribeca to
Morningside Heights, in the hopes of making a year's worth of income from one month's worth of selling.

A scruffy bunch, the tree salespeople were. Dungarees and
Carhartt jackets were their uniform. Some arrived in caravans,
like Gypsies, parked their trailers by the curb, and lived out
December in the vans' cramped chill, carbon monoxide pumping
out along with the meager heat. Some would stick a huge illuminated Santa or snowman on the van roof.

When it came to vending Christmas trees, Christy had no
peer. He used to leave his family behind and travel alone—set up
his stand on the corner in Chelsea, string up white lights to show
off his trees with their salt-sparkle, and use his silver Irish tongue
to sell every last one at top dollar in time to get home on Christmas Eve—laden with sugarplums, walnuts, fine chocolates, and
cheeses from the best Manhattan markets; golden-haired dolls,
tin soldiers, silver skates, and Flexible Flyer sleds for Bridget and
Danny; soft red wool sweaters and fine cream silk nightgowns for
Mary. Why not spend some of the profits on his family? He'd
made plenty off the glamorous people of New York City.

He'd go home and tell everyone about it, tell Danny what he
had to look forward to. "We'll be partners, you and I," Christy had
said. "When you get old enough, you're going to own half this
farm. Study up in school, son. You can't take farming for granted.
You've got to be a scientist—learn all about weather patterns,
and soil acidity, and grubs."

"You're saying it takes book knowledge? To be a farmer?" Mary
had asked, laughing. Christy had held in his hurt—she'd never

appreciated the skills it took. Her father had done two years of college in Halifax, worked in the front office of a lobster company, and Christy knew she had similar designs for their son.

"That, and instincts," Christy had replied, aware that Danny was listening, wanting him to be proud of his tree-farming heritage. "Running the land takes the best we have—all of it! It's magical work, it is, to make Christmas trees grow out of nothing much more than sun and dirt."

"And precipitation," Danny had said. "Moderate rainfall and occluded fronts." Christy had laughed affectionately at the big words and the serious look in his boy's eyes.

But after Mary's death after a heart attack four years ago, he had had to take the children with him to New York. Danny had been twelve then, and Bridget eight. The school always gave them permission, along with a month's worth of lessons and homework to do while their father hustled the trees. Danny's eyes had just about sprung out of his head, the first time he saw the city: the towers, bridges, fancy stores.

"This is New York City?" he'd asked that first year, mesmerized. "It's so—big, Pa! Like a forest of buildings, all lit up."

"Just don't lose sight of the farm," Christy had warned.

"Never, Pa," Danny had said.

So Christy would rent two rooms at Mrs. Quinn's boardinghouse right there on Ninth Avenue, where he could keep an eye on the trees. A big room for him and Danny, a smaller one for Bridget—he could afford it, because his blue and white spruces, Douglas firs, and Scotch pines were the best, and he could always get the rich New Yorkers to pay half again as much as they would for the trees on other street corners. He would rig a chain around the trees, so no one could steal them—and he'd sleep with one eye open, besides. He'd put nothing past New Yorkers—the street people would take anything, and the moneyed people would get away with what they could.

"It's how the rich get richer," he'd say.

Mary used to chide him for his cynical attitude about the wealthy denizens of Manhattan. "Christy, they're paying our way the year round. They've been meeting the mortgage on our land, and they're going to pay for college—if you'll ever let Danny off the farm long enough to go. So don't go putting your mouth on them!"

"Ah, they've got so much money, they don't even notice the air they breathe," Christy said, ignoring her dig. "They don't notice the snow, except to complain that it ruins their expensive shoes. They're so busy rushing to get out of the wind, they forget to feel the sting on their faces, letting them know they're alive."

"Well, you're happy enough to take their dollars," she'd say.

"That I am," Christy would laugh. "Believe me, they've enough so they won't miss it. If I doubled my prices, I'd probably sell out twice as fast—the rich people love to spend their money, and if something costs them a lot, it gives them a reason to swagger."

"You're a scandal, Christy Byrne," Mary would say, shaking her head. "Selling Christmas trees with that kind of a mentality is some kind of a sin, it is. It's going to get you in trouble—mark my words."

Mary's family had been comfortable, and she'd never gone to bed hungry. What did she know? He'd ask himself in the tree fields wet with rain, the short, enchanted Nova Scotia summers when he'd walk along the crystal-cool streams, feeling the rapture of summer's breeze as he pruned the spruces' golden growth into Christmas tree shapes, calculating the handsome dividends they'd bring in December.

This year, with the power saws roaring like demons, spitting out wood chips in their vicious, hellish destruction of nature's best, Christy knew that Mary had been right. Last winter Manhattan—for all the money it had given him over the years—had exacted the greatest price imaginable, interest on all his profits, on what Mary had called his greed, compounded beyond comprehension: New York City had taken his only son.

Three years of city lights had proven too much temptation for the teenage boy. And last Christmas Eve, after a banner season of tree selling, Danny had informed his father he wasn't returning home to Nova Scotia with him and Bridget. He was going to stay in New York—find a job, make his way.

"What do you mean," Christy had asked, " 'make your way'?"

"Let me go, Pa—I can't talk about it anymore! You don't get it!"

"Staying in New York? Are you mad, Danny?"

The tension between them was terrible. Christy grabbed his sleeve, felt Danny pulling away—literally yanking his arm back. And that made Christy hold on tighter.

"There's no talking about this," Danny said. "There never was. It's just your way, Pa—the farm. I have something I want to do right now. It's my dream, Pa. And I have to follow it! You've taught me not to waste time talking when work needs to be done."

Danny was serious, and he was right: Christy had taught him that very thing. Talking took up too much time, when there was a whole farm that needed tending to. Of course, what Danny didn't know was that Christy was *afraid* of talking. He feared his children asking him questions he didn't know the answers to, telling him things that would stir up his emotions. He loved his kids with passion beyond words.

Now Danny was staring at his father with the resolute, not-to-be-deterred eyes of a dreamer. Christy was scathed, wounded. How could his son have a dream, something that would keep him here, in New York, that Christy knew nothing about? Deep down he knew enough to blame himself—he hadn't exactly been an open listener. But more to the point, how could he leave Danny alone in this place? It couldn't happen. Christy tightened his grip. Danny broke free.

Their first father-son face-off—right then and there.

They'd had a fistfight, there on the street corner—Christy had scuffled with his own son and, scrambling to hold on to him, had torn his jacket—the new down parka he'd bought for Danny at the start of the season. Feathers flying, Danny's elbow accidentally cracking Christy's nose, blood flowing as Christy tried to hold Danny still—if he could only talk to the boy, keep him from running—he could get him to see reason. There they were, struggling on the snowy sidewalk, Bridget screaming for the fighting to stop.

The police were called. Squad cars had converged, sirens blaring. The fight had torn down Christy's white lights, and now they lay tangled on the sidewalk, illuminating the bloody snow. One cop had grabbed Christy, handcuffed his hands behind his back—and Danny had used that opportunity to escape.

Christy's last glimpse of his boy had been of him illuminated by blue police strobes, dodging through the crowd of gawkers, white goose down spewing from his ripped jacket like a snow squall.

"It's frigid out," Christy had said to the officer booking him at the station. "He's going to be hungry and cold, with his parka ruined."

"That's the Christmas spirit. Maybe you should have thought of that before you beat him up," the cop said. His name was Officer Rip Collins.

Christy was too proud to protest, to spill his true feelings of grief and terror, to a New York police officer. What did the cop know? What did anyone from this brutal, blazing, glittering city know? With all its false light, its temples to greed, its foolish people so easily tricked into paying small fortunes for simple pine trees?

ROR—released on his own recognizance—Christy left the precinct house. He'd returned to the boardinghouse. His blood was roaring through his veins—he was hoping against hope that his son would be there. But all he'd found was Bridget, sitting on the bed, her face streaked with tears.

Christy had packed up his daughter and, with the heaviest heart imaginable, gone home to Canada. There was a hearing scheduled for March, but Officer Collins spoke to the ADA in charge, telling him what had really happened. And with Danny nowhere to be found—in spite of Collins and other city cops looking for him—the charge against Christy had been thrown out. Where he should have been relieved, Christy was instead soul-sick; to the New York police and court system, his family had become just another statistic of domestic trouble, and his son had become just one more street kid.

Now, one year later, the pickup was packed and ready for him and his daughter to return to New York. They'd had just one post-card from Danny, of the Brooklyn Bridge, with not a clue in the message about where he was living or how he was really faring. Just the brash words: "I'm doing grand—don't worry about me."

Not a word about missing Christy or Bridget or their thirty acres of fir trees on the edge of the world. The boy had come from a magical northern land, inhabited by bald eagles, black bears, red and silver foxes, and great horned owls. He had left it for the urban caverns of New York, populated by players and hustlers. Christy hated the place with a passion, never wanted to set foot in the city again.

But he knew he had to. Had to set up his trees on the same Chelsea corner, had to string up his lights so they'd set the salt crystals on the trees' needles gleaming and entice the customers, had to cock his smile and throw the charm, had to sell out his evergreens and put money in the bank. But most of all, had to be in the same place he always was, so Danny would know where to find him.

"Come on, Bridget," he shouted up the stairs. She appeared at the top, dragging another huge suitcase behind her.

"What's that?" he asked.

"It's my things, Pa," she said.

"Your things are in the truck, Bridget! We're only going for twenty-four days. What've you got in there?"

"Party clothes, Pa." Her green eyes were shimmering.

Christy stared up at her. She was almost thirteen now, a young lady. She'd curled her pretty brown hair by herself, tied it with a burgundy velvet ribbon she'd found somewhere. What the hell did she think she'd be needing with party clothes? Christy worked all day every day until his trees were sold.

"Bridget," he started.

"Danny's coming back to us, and we're going to take him somewhere special to celebrate."

"Leave the case here. Be a good girl, and let's get going."

"I've seen it on TV, a program about New York City, Pa," she said, the words spilling out as she started to bump the huge suitcase down the stairs. "Fancy places we've never gone to yet. Places Danny would love—palaces, Pa! All with crystal and gold, and with Christmas trees bigger than the oldest ones on our mountain, all covered with garlands and tiny lights. Like a fairyland, honest! Girls having tea with their fathers in places like that, and boys all dressed up with ties, everyone so happy and celebrating the holiday together, Pa."

"That's not how you celebrate a holiday," Christy said gruffly.

"But we have to do something wonderful, when Danny comes back to us!"

"Get in the truck now, Bridget," he said, pointing with force at the front door. She scowled, limping past him under the weight of her case. Reluctantly he lifted it for her, into the compartment behind the seat. They climbed in and slammed the doors.

Christy had warmed up the cab for her, but he didn't suppose she'd noticed. That's okay, he told himself. One of the ways he measured that he'd been a good provider was that his kids never commented when they were warm enough, or when their stomachs weren't hurting from hunger; they took their comfort for granted, which was just what children should do. Christy wouldn't even try to force Danny to come home—he swore it to himself.

He just had to make sure his boy wasn't hungry. And to hear if he'd gotten any closer to his "dream." Looking down the farm's hillside toward the sea, he wondered how any dream could be better than this—this was all Danny's and Bridget's. If he could harness the wind, capture the sunlight, he would. And he would give it to his kids.

"We're going to see Danny now, Pa," Bridget said. "You should be happy."

He'd been grimacing. He tried to relax his face, so as not to upset her. But he hurt so much inside; the harder he tried to look calm, the more he felt her hopes rising, and with the one single postcard from her brother, the deeper he felt the agony.

The hired eighteen-wheeler he'd loaded with the trees was waiting at the end of their road, great clouds of exhaust billowing into the cold clear air over the Gulf of St. Lawrence. When the driver spotted Christy's pickup, he blasted the horn.

Christy pulled up behind the long-hauler, and they set off for their two-day journey to New York City.

2

*T*he holiday season started earlier and earlier every year. Once it had been the day after Thanksgiving—the unofficial day that Manhattan would start to put up decorations. Now, Catherine Tierney thought, it seemed to happen in October—even as the greenmarkets were overflowing with pumpkins and grocery shelves were laden with Halloween candy. The city began to dress in its winter finery, weighting Catherine's soul a little more each day.

All through November Catherine had watched tiny, twinkling white lights appearing in midtown shop windows. Bell-ringing Santas would clang away, standing in front of Lord & Taylor and Macy's as passersby stuffed their cast-iron kettles with dollar bills.

Salvation Army bands would start playing "Silent Night" and "God Rest Ye Merry, Gentlemen" outside Saks Fifth Avenue to the captive audience of people lined up to see the famous holiday windows. Squeezing past the crowd, Catherine kept her face stoic, so no one could see what the carols were doing to her heart.

By the first week of December, the city was in full holiday swing. Hotels were filled with shoppers and people in town to see City Ballet's *Nutcracker*, Radio City's Christmas show, Handel's *Messiah*, and of course, the Rockefeller Center tree. The avenues crept with yellow cabs, and on her way to the subway, Catherine would be jostled by wall-to-wall people inching along in their thick coats.

Catherine Tierney worked as a librarian in a private library owned by the Rheinbeck Corporation. The Rheinbecks had made their fortune in banking, and now real estate; they were philanthropists who supported education and the arts. The library occupied the fifty-fourth floor of the Rheinbeck building at Fifth Avenue and Fifty-ninth Street, just across the Grand Army Plaza from Central Park.

The Rheinbeck Tower was fantastically gothic, with arched windows, pinnacles, flying buttresses, finials, and gargoyles, rising sixty stories to an ornate green cast-stone point. The offices, and Catherine's library, had astonishing views of the park—the eight-hundred-and-forty-three-acre green haven in the city's midst.

The building's facade was lit year round, Paris style, with gold light. For the holidays, the illumination changed to red and green. The spectacular four-story barrel-vaulted lobby accommodated an enormous tree, covered with colored balls and lights. The

Byzantine-style mosaics glistened like real gold, and evergreen roping garlanded the frescoed second-floor balconies.

Choirs sang carols in the lobby at lunchtime, a different city school group every day. That afternoon Catherine returned to work with her sandwich, and she paused to listen. The children's voices joined together, sweet and pure.

One little girl in the back row was off-key. Catherine watched her, head thrown back with brown braids hanging down, mouth open wide, singing her heart out. The choir director shot the girl an ice-cold look and a hand signal, and suddenly the girl stopped—her eyes wide with dismay as they flooded with tears. Catherine's stomach churned at the sight. She had to walk away, hurry upstairs, to keep from getting involved—telling the girl to keep singing, berating the director for squashing her spirit. That's what Brian would have done.

The look in that girl's eyes was with Catherine all day. From "Joy to the World" to the shock of being silenced. She felt the child's shame in her own heart and for the rest of the day found it almost impossible to concentrate on her project—pulling up material from the archives on stone angels and gargoyles on buildings in Manhattan. She couldn't wait to get home and put this day behind her.

At five-thirty, Catherine locked up and headed for the subway. She lived in Chelsea. Situated west of Sixth Avenue, roughly between Fourteenth and Twenty-third Streets, that part of town had its own personality. Eighth Avenue was playful, shop and restaurant windows decorated with wreaths of red peppers, Santa in a sleigh drawn by eight flamingos, candles shaped like the Grinch and Betty Lou Who.

The side streets had a nineteenth-century feel, with many Italianate and Greek Revival brownstones set back from the sidewalk, their yards enclosed by ornate wrought-iron gates and lit by reproduction gas lamps.

Some residents decorated for the holidays as if Chelsea were still part of the estate of Clement Clarke Moore, author of "A Visit from St. Nicholas"—with English holly, laurel, and evergreen roping, Della Robbia wreaths, red ribbons, and gold and silver balls. It was so understated that if you didn't want to notice, you didn't have to.

The minute Catherine stepped off the E train at Twenty-third and Eighth, she breathed a sigh of relief. The buildings were low, and she could see the sky. The air was frigid, crystal clear, and so dry that it hurt to draw a breath. She wore stylish boots and a short black wool coat; her knees and toes were cold as she hurried across West Twenty-second Street, on her way home.

At Ninth Avenue she turned south. The Christmas tree man had arrived again—she stopped short when she saw him there; her pulse felt like galloping horses. For a second, she considered crossing the street to avoid having to look him in the eye.

She had witnessed the scene with his son last year—and she had doubted that he would come back. But here he was, just setting up his display of spruce and pine, making the sidewalk smell like a mountain forest. The trees stretched a quarter of the way down the block of small stores—an antiquarian book dealer, two avant-garde clothes designers, a new bakery, a florist, and Chez Liz.

In a brilliant fit of quirkiness possible only in Chelsea, Lizzie sold hats, which she made, along with hard-to-find poetry books and antique tea sets. When she was in the mood, she would set the mahogany table inside with her Spode and Wedgwood china and serve tea to whoever walked in. Catherine felt so nervous, seeing the man, she dove at Lizzie's door to duck inside. The shop was warmly lit by silk-shaded lamps, but the door was locked—Lizzie and Lucy had already left.

"She closed early tonight—left with the little one," the tree man said, leaning against the makeshift rack of raw pine boards that held numerous wreaths, sprays, and garlands. "I asked her, beautiful as she looked in that black velvet hat with the one peacock feather sticking up, was she going to the opera? Or maybe something at the Irish Repertory Theater?" He nodded toward Twenty-second Street, where the theater was located.

"Hmm," Catherine said, her palms damp inside her gloves, wanting to get away.

"She told me that she was going to 'the banquet.'"

Catherine hid a smile. Lizzie *would* say that.

"What I think she'd say to you, if she was here," he said, stamping his feet to keep them warm, his Irish brogue coming out in clouds, "is that you should buy a nice fresh Nova Scotia Christmas tree from me. And a wreath, for your front door. I see you walk by every day, and you look to me like someone who would fancy white spruce..."

The man was tall, with broad shoulders under a rugged canvas jacket. His hair was light brown, but even in the dark she could see it was grayer than it had been the year before. He had been warming his hands by a kerosene heater; he stepped closer to Catherine, and after what had happened last year, she leaned sharply back.

"I don't want a white spruce," Catherine said.

"No? Then maybe a hardy blue—"

"Or any other tree," she said. She had had a headache ever since the carol incident in the lobby, and she just wanted to get home.

"Just look at these needles," he said, brushing a branch with one bare hand. "They're as fresh as the day the trees were cut—they'll never fall. And see how they glisten? That's the Cape Breton salt spray...you know, it's said that starlight gets caught in the branches, and..."

He paused in the midst of the sentence, trailing off as if he'd forgotten what he was saying or lost the heart for his spiel. Catherine had noticed his blue eyes sparkling during hard sells in the past, but tonight they were as dull as last week's snow. They held her gaze for a moment, then looked down at the ground. She felt her heart pounding as she kept her face neutral so he couldn't read her thoughts.

"Thank you anyway," Catherine said, edging away.

As she walked home, she felt doubly uncomfortable. She was still upset about the little girl, and now she had to face the fact that the tree man would be in her neighborhood till Christmas Eve, and she'd probably have to change her route. She wondered whether his daughter had come with him this year. She hoped his son was somewhere warm. Her nose and fingertips stung with the cold. A December wind blew off the Hudson River, and when she turned right onto West Twentieth Street, she saw little clouds of vapor around the gaslights of Cushman Row.

In spite of the brutal chill, she paused to stare at the penumbra around one flickering lamp. The globe of light might have been due to moisture blowing off the river, forecasting a storm like a ring around the moon. It reminded Catherine of a ghost. It's a harbinger, she thought and hoped as she clenched her freezing hands and walked on.

Chelsea was haunted at Christmas. Or at least one room in one townhouse, in the very middle of Cushman Row. Like its neighbors—other brick Greek Revivals with tall brownstone steps, pocket-sized yards, and ornate cast-iron railings—the house where Catherine lived had been built in 1840 by Don Alonzo Cushman, a friend of Clement Clark Moore.

Catherine paused, holding on to the iron railing and gazing at the brick house, four stories up to the small attic windows. Leaded glass, encircled by plaster wreaths of laurel leaves, they were one of the house's prettiest, most charming features. The tiny panes of glass gave onto the sky. Strangers walking by often stopped to peer upward at those mysterious little windows.

People always made assumptions about other people's lives. Catherine thought of passing strangers imagining happiness inside. Perhaps they gazed at the pretty townhouse and pictured elegant dinner parties going on. They would probably assume it belonged to a loving couple with brilliant children—perhaps their playroom was up in the attic, behind those small wreathed windows.

Why shouldn't they imagine such things? Catherine had herself, at one time. Her eyes on those windows, she felt a cold tingle down her spine. It gripped her as if she were being electrocuted, wouldn't let her move or look away. There were ghosts in the street tonight; she closed her eyes tight, trying to feel the one she loved, beg it to visit her tonight in the attic.

The season was here again. December, once such a source of joy and delight, had become a time of sorrow and pain—Catherine didn't celebrate at all. It brought nothing but sad memories—she wanted to rush through the pre-holiday craziness.

Shaking herself free of the shiver and such thoughts, she ran up the front stairs to close the door behind her and pull the covers over her head.

A few blocks away Lizzie Donnelly stood behind the food table, wearing her dark-red brocade cape and black velvet hat. Steam rose from the food, misting her harlequin glasses. She had to keep taking them off and handing them to her nine-year-old daughter, Lucy, to wipe them, to make sure she wasn't giving anyone too little food—not that she really had to worry: her clients would let her know.

"Thanks, honey," Lizzie said.

"No problem, Mom. Keep dishing up the supper, though— everyone's hungry," Lucy said.

"Hi Joe, hey there Billy, hello Ruthie, what's going on Maurice, are you being good, don't want any coal in your stocking this year, right?" Lizzie kept up the banter, filling their plates with tonight's delicacy—pot roast, mashed potatoes, and peas and carrots. The priest passed through the crowded room of St. Lucy's soup kitchen on his way from the rectory to the church.

"Hey, Father," several called.

"God bless, God bless," he said, his clothes a black blur as he hurried along.

"What'll you have?" Lizzie asked the next person in line. "May I suggest the pot roast? The chef has really outdone himself today."

Lizzie volunteered here twice a week. She had been baptized

at St. Lucy's. So had her daughter, whom she had named after the church and Saint Lucy herself. She and her best friend, Catherine, had made their first communion together. They had gone all through grammar school, middle school, and high school together. Three years earlier Catherine had asked her to take Brian's place at the soup kitchen. *We have so much, and we have to give back,* Brian had once said. Lizzie had agreed—how could she not? And so they had started.

Now Lizzie was alone with her ladle. Since Brian's funeral, Catherine had refused to set foot in a church, even St. Lucy's. Lizzie tried arguing, saying that technically the soup kitchen was in the parish hall, but even after three years Catherine was still too raw to listen to reason. Lizzie always expected her best friend's heart to melt a little at Christmas, but in fact, it hardened.

"Peas and carrots, red and green," Lucy said, standing off to the side.

"A little Christmas cheer," Lizzie said, starting to sweat under her cape.

"Hey Lucy, hi Lizzie" came Harry's voice.

"Harry!" Lucy said.

"Where've you been, Harry?" Lizzie asked, whipping around the table to give the tall man a hug. He let her crash into his body and actually held on for an instant, then pushed her away.

"Hey, knock it off," he said, eyes darting back and forth at the men in line and hunched over their food at the long tables. "The guys'll see."

"So let them," Lizzie said. "They'd all trade in their rice pudding for one hug from me. Seriously, where have you been? We were getting worried about you."

"A little of this, a little of that," he said.

"What does that mean?" Lucy asked.

"It sounds dangerous," Lizzie said wryly. "Especially coming from you, Harry." She scanned his face for clues to what was really going on. The street aged people beyond their years. Their eyes grew dull, their faces became lined from the sun and wind and stress, their bones curved and shrank from bad nutrition. Drugs became some people's way out, their magic carpet to a better place, and the ticket sometimes cost their lives. Not Harry, not so far, Lizzie thought. If anything, his eyes looked brighter and sharper.

"I've got to get going," he said, pulling an envelope from the back pocket of his torn and dirty jeans. "Will you give this to C?"

"Sure," Lizzie said, accepting the message and giving him a curious look. "What's inside?"

"She'll know," he said.

"She and I are having breakfast at the diner tomorrow. Why don't you meet us there and give it to her yourself?" Lizzie asked, hoping to trick him into a free meal.

"I have an appointment," he said, eyes dropping furtively. The way he said it made Lizzie's stomach fall. She didn't know what he did for money, and she realized she honestly didn't want to know.

"Will you have a plate of food?" she asked. "It's good tonight."

He glanced at the meat and potatoes, and Lucy thrust a plate into his hands. Lizzie filled it up, piling on some extra pot roast. He sat at one end of a table and started to eat. Lizzie watched with satisfaction. He finished in record time, cleared his plate, and stopped to say good-bye.

"Thanks," he said.

"Anytime. That's what we're here for."

"You won't forget to give that thing to C, will you?"

"No. You can count on me."

Lizzie leaned forward to give him another hug—she was under orders to do that as often as possible. Lucy did the same. But he was true to his name and disappeared into the crowd of people congregating at the door—savoring the last moments of warmth before heading back out into the cold night.

"Where's he going, Mom?"

"To the shelter, honey. At least I hope so."

Lizzie could only watch him leave. She tucked his envelope under her cape, wondering what it contained, and with a strange sense of melancholy smiled at her daughter and went back to presiding over the banquet.

Bridget Byrne sat at the end of the sofa, trying to do her schoolwork. She had the TV on low, so no one else could hear—she wasn't allowed to watch until she had finished the assignments that her teacher in Nova Scotia had sent for that day. Not that there were too many around to notice, but Bridget could hear Mrs. Quinn in her rooms, shuffling around. Danny used to call her "old eagle eye," because she was always watching.

That was one way Bridget and Danny were different. While Danny had always hated being supervised, Bridget loved it. It made her feel good to have someone pay attention, even the elderly owner of the boardinghouse. She felt that her mother would approve of Mrs. Quinn and her concern. In other years Danny had looked after her, too. They sometimes made friends, but it was hard in New York in the winter. Kids mostly stayed inside. Danny and Bridget had had each other.

In spite of missing Danny, Bridget liked it here. The heat rattled in the pipes, in the most comforting way, warming every room through. The wallpaper in the common room was old and yellowed, patterned with roses and forget-me-nots. The ceiling had a brownish cast, and Mrs. Quinn had told her it was from years of smoke. "This was a sailors' boardinghouse, darling," she'd said. "Longshoremen, stevedores, crew from the boats that stopped at the Chelsea docks, going back nearly two hundred years. They all smoked."

Bridget had just listened, not letting on that some of the smoke was from her own brother—Danny had sometimes snuck a cigarette when their father was out selling trees and Mrs. Quinn was watching one of her programs.

Right now Bridget's attention was riveted to the TV. The *Live at Five* newscaster stood in front of the tree at Rockefeller Center, just thirty blocks away from where Bridget sat.

"In two days, thirty thousand bulbs will be lit on this eighty-foot Norway spruce from Wall, New Jersey," the reporter said as the camera showed the beautiful dark tree silhouetted by city lights. Clips were shown of the tree being hoisted into place last Thursday. When the camera started panning the crowd, Bridget literally dove at the screen.

Some people held signs reading, "Hello to Brisbane!" "Hi Mom and Dad in Columbus," "Happy Holidays to everyone in Louisville!" Bridget scanned every face, her pulse racing. She knew the person she was looking for would not be holding a sign. He would be standing in the background, trying to hide. He would be breathing in the smell of pine, gazing at the sharp black-green needles, at the bark glistening with golden sap, at the fierce point aimed straight up at the stars. He was the big tree's guardian and shepherd.

Now the news cut to a fire on the Upper West Side, and Bridget closed her eyes, thinking about her brother. Danny had always believed that Christmas trees had souls. He'd always been fascinated by weather, and he'd make up stories about how the snow angels breathed life into the trees. Sunlight produced chlorophyll, creating cloaks of green needles. "They've got spirits of their own, Bridey," he'd say. "Every last one of them. They're alive, roots going down into the earth and branches reaching up to the sky."

"And we cut them down," Bridget had said, stricken. "And kill them!"

"Nah, don't think like that. The trees drop seeds in the ground before the harvest—to make sure they carry on—depending on precipitation and prevailing winds, of course."

"Danny . . . not weather again. Tell me about the *trees!*"

"But the weather says it all, Bridey! Remember all that heavy rain last week, how we had to wait for the low pressure system to slowly drift off the coast, bringing a slow end to the rainfall? Well, even after that, we had flash flood warnings, and NEXRAD said—"

"Jeez, Danny. Not NEXRAD. I don't care about weather reports. I want to hear about the trees. The snow angels bring them to life, and the sun cloaks them in green needles, and we *kill* them!"

"The trees do die, it's true. The minute the saws cut through their trunks—"

"That's terrible," Bridget had cried.

"But the thing is, Bridey," Danny said, "they come back to life."

"How?"

"Well, when the lights go on."

"When the—"

"You know. When a person takes the tree home and puts lights on it."

"When they love it enough?"

"Something like that."

Danny was too tough to admit he was doing it, but Bridey had seen him looking over their father's trees before they were bought. He would stand in their shadow, the air sharp and cold, waiting for someone to pass by and take one home. Perhaps, like Bridey, he'd be dreaming of the great apartments—high in a skyscraper, cozy in a townhouse—and the brilliant possibilities that could happen here in New York City.

"Just look up there," he'd say to Bridget, pointing up at the Empire State Building, lit up green and red for the holidays. "What kind of great city would paint the sky like that? Do you know the electricity it takes? You could light all of Nova Scotia with the power it takes to do that."

"You wouldn't like living here, Danny! A month is one thing, but you'd never last longer than that. There are no trees here, except for our cut ones and the skinny ones growing out of the sidewalks. No forests. Where would you find owls and hawks here? Where could you watch storms coming?"

"I didn't say I wanted to live here. But you're wrong about the trees, and nature, and storm watching. New York has it all. There're places," Danny had said in his secretive way, making Bridget wonder where he went on his wanderings. Just then *Live at Five* ended and *News 4 New York* came on, with more shots of

Rockefeller Center. Snow flurries falling, people skating on the ice, the statue of Prometheus gleaming gold behind them, the Christmas tree dark and majestic, rising above hordes of people waving at the camera.

Now, eyes glued to her TV, Bridget prayed to see her brother. He hadn't come to find her yet—and she and her father had been back in New York for a whole day. Her fingernails dug into her palms. "Danny, Danny, I have to see you," she said. She stared into the crowd of happy faces, people visiting from all over, here to experience the Christmas magic of New York City: magic so powerful, it had captured her brother, taken him from his family.

"Where are you, Danny?" she asked the television set with her throat aching as she watched the snow catching in the spruce needles and thought of her brother's snow angels. "Will you come back to us? You *have* to . . ."

The tree was dark. Its spirit was dead and wouldn't come alive for two days—until the lights were lit. Bridget knew that her brother was there. He might not come back to Chelsea right away—he'd be remembering how mad their father had been last year. But when he did return, Bridget was ready to celebrate. She'd brought all her finery. The whole family would go to the Plaza for tea—it would be wonderful and special. But until then Bridget imagined him standing guard over the big tree in Rockefeller Center. Watching it get covered in snow . . .

She was so intent, watching for Danny on TV, that she didn't hear the footsteps in the alley outside. One of the garbage cans rattled—that got her attention, and she looked up. She heard a scratching sound, like fingernails scrabbling on wood, but she attributed it to Mrs. Quinn's little dog, Murphy. Murphy was always wanting to go out . . . In fact, there she was, barking now.

"Did you hear that?" Mrs. Quinn asked, walking straight through the sitting room, Murphy at her heels. Murphy jumped up on the chair beside the window, acting very brave and barking ferociously, as if she were a German shepherd instead of a tiny Yorkshire terrier.

"I didn't hear anything," Bridget said, eyes on the screen.

"Those street people, going through the garbage," she said, getting started on one of her pet peeves. "Looking for empty cans to return again. I wouldn't mind them so much, if they wouldn't leave such a mess." Just then she must have noticed the TV turned on. "Now, what's this, young lady? Aren't you supposed to be doing homework?"

Bridget couldn't reply. She didn't dare turn around. If she did, Mrs. Quinn would see that her eyes were red and full of tears. Didn't Mrs. Quinn know that Danny was a street person now? Where was he sleeping? What was he eating? The shepherd of the trees, the boy who loved to watch storms, needed to stay strong and to be safe.

Oh, Danny, Bridget thought silently, tears starting to flow as she gazed at the crowd on TV.

3

*E*very Thursday morning Catherine and Lizzie met for breakfast at Moonstruck, the diner on the southwest corner of Twenty-third Street and Ninth Avenue. On her way there, Catherine passed the tree man. A light snow had fallen during the night, blanketing Chelsea in white.

The man, unaware of Catherine approaching, stood very still, holding a cardboard coffee cup. She saw the steam rising, imagined the cup warming his hands. He was gazing at his trees—covered with snow, silver and white ice crystals glinting in the early morning sun as if the pines were still growing on the farm in Nova Scotia.

"Good morning to you. Have you ever seen anything more beautiful?" he asked as she drew near.

"Morning," she said, picking up the pace.

"Maybe you'll buy one on your way home tonight!" he called after her.

By the time Catherine got to Moonstruck, Lizzie had already dropped Lucy off at school and was in a booth by the window, reading the *Times*. She wore a dark green satin vest over a sleek maroon challis dress. Her green Bavarian-style hat matched the vest and had a small red silk poinsettia pinned to the taffeta band. Catherine pulled off her black coat, scarf, and gloves, hung them on the wall.

"Now, tell me about the message you left on my answering machine," Lizzie said, the instant Catherine sat down. "About what happened yesterday—the *caroling incident*."

Catherine heard the slight tease in Lizzie's invisible italics but ignored it and ran through the story of what she'd seen in the lobby of her building yesterday—the little girl singing off-key. "You should have seen her face—the color just drained out of it. She was so upset—all the other kids just kept singing their hearts out, and she just stood there trying not to cry. I wanted to literally wring the choir director's neck."

"But you didn't?"

"No."

"And you didn't rescue the girl and take her to a better choir that would appreciate her more?"

"No."

"My, you're making progress!" Lizzie said, grinning as the waiter came to take their order. They both got the same things: coffee, fresh orange juice, and toasted poppyseed bagels with butter.

"It made me think of Lucy," Catherine said.

"Lucy would have ignored her and started singing twice as loudly."

"And it made me think of Brian."

"Everything makes you think of Brian," Lizzie replied softly.

"He wouldn't have been able to stand by, you know? He never could take any kind of injustice. Even in a choir." Catherine closed her eyes, to conjure up Brian's face. She saw his bright green eyes, dark hair, square jaw. She saw him in his suit and tie, charging in to save the day. He had left his lucrative law practice to work for an education advocacy program because he believed in helping people, and she had fallen in love with him because . . . he was Brian.

"Cath, you have to stop this," Lizzie said.

"It was the way the choir lady gestured at her," Catherine said. "So sharp and mean—she made the little girl cry. What's the point of leading a group of kids, helping them to shine, to sing, if you're not going to do it nicely?"

"I know," Lizzie said. "Sounds as if she's missing the spirit of the season."

Their breakfasts came, and they started to eat. Catherine thought about Lizzie's words: the spirit of the season. Catherine used to have it, but it had been in short supply these last three years. As she chewed her bagel, her gaze drifted out the window, to the Christmas tree man.

"Have you seen the tree guy?" Catherine asked. "He's back—there he is, right in front of your shop."

"Sure, I've noticed him. How can I not? He's hot—I sit in my shop and stare out the window, picturing him without his jacket on. Without his shirt on. Cutting pine trees in the burning Nova Scotia sun. His muscular forearms getting all nice and tense, sawing branches. Sweaty . . ."

"Stop it."

Lizzie waved her hand. "I'm single, why shouldn't I?"

Catherine didn't really have an answer for that. Lizzie had just broken up with a man she'd loved for too long. He hadn't wanted to marry her, take on raising Lucy, a readymade family, a fact that Catherine thought made him dumb, bad, and foolish.

"What am I supposed to do? Sit around and pretend to *be* a tree? Made of wood and bark and needles? Instead of a woman with hormones and emotions and a need to be noticed? Does he check you out when you walk by?"

"The tree man?"

"Whose name we both know is Christopher Byrne, by the way. But yes—the tree man."

"I guess. He wants to sell me a tree."

Lizzie tilted her head. With her hat already fashionably askew, her head looked as if it were about to fall onto her shoulder.

"You could be kind to him, oh you of the bleeding heart."

"It's easier not to. All I have to do is remember last year."

Lizzie shook her head. "He tried to hold on to his son. He didn't want his kid to stay behind in New York and become a street urchin. Do you ever think of it that way?"

"Brian would have stepped right in and broken up the fight," Catherine said, and just saying his name filled her with so much emotion, she had to pause and let it pass.

Lizzie let a few seconds pass, and then she spoke. "We're coming up on Brian's third anniversary, I know."

"I saw the first ghosts last night," Catherine said.

"They always come the first of December," Lizzie said, "at the same time as the Christmas trees."

Catherine glanced out the diner window. The sun had risen above the low buildings and was melting the snow on Christopher Byrne's row of trees. Maybe that was why she didn't like seeing him—his arrival always reminded her of losing Brian.

"Father Cusack asked for you last night," Lizzie said, changing gears. "He said the soup kitchen needs you."

Catherine missed standing in the big kitchen at St. Lucy's, helping to cook and serve meals, feed the hungry. She and Brian had done it together, every Sunday night, since they'd first gotten married, nine years ago. Then, when he left Slade & Linden to start work at the Family Orchard Program, he had more work than he could handle. Catherine had understood, so she had enlisted Lizzie to join her on Sundays.

"I pass by St. Lucy's and think of our wedding," Catherine said. "The most beautiful day ever, so full of love that was supposed to last forever. Blessed by Father Cusack. And as he said, by God and St. Lucy and all the angels and saints. I think of that day, and all the other happy days—Lucy's christening, with me and Brian as godparents . . . and then I think of Brian's funeral."

"I know, darling," Lizzie said.

"I'll never set foot in there again."

"Okay."

"Right now, at work for Mr. Rheinbeck, I have to find images of all the angels in New York architecture—statues, cornices, building ornaments—and even *that* makes me mad. Where were the angels when Brian died?"

Lizzie didn't reply. She just sat there across the booth listening. Catherine blinked back tears. This was such a hard time of year. Glancing out the window, she saw a customer stopping by the trees. Everyone wanted to put up holiday decorations, sing Christmas carols, feel happy. But how was that possible, when terrible things happened to the people they loved? Catherine wiped her eyes and wondered.

Checking her watch, Catherine realized it was getting late. She had to get to work, so she counted out the money for her part of the bill.

"Oh," Lizzie said, rummaging through her bag, "I almost forgot."

"What's this?" Catherine asked, staring at the envelope Lizzie put on the table. It was plain white except for the letter C.

"It's from a secret admirer," Lizzie said.

"Harry?" Catherine asked, smiling in spite of herself.

"Houdini himself. You'll have to let me know what he says—I was dying to open the envelope."

"I will," Catherine said, walking with her best friend up to the cash register. "I tell you everything."

"About most things," Lizzie said as they walked outside, onto the street. "But when it comes to Harry, I know you have your secrets."

Catherine just smiled and gave Lizzie a hug and kiss, then hurried toward the subway. The sidewalk was still snowy in patches, and she nearly slipped. She ran down the stairs and jumped onto a crowded E train, just as it was about to pull away. Jostled by other straphangers, she slung her arm around the pole and managed to pull the letter open.

It was one sheet of white paper, completely blank except for one line:

"Will you let me in?"

Catherine closed her eyes, and as the subway rattled beneath the city streets, she knew she would.

Christy Byrne was out working in the frigid air, wide awake in that jangling way he always felt when he hadn't gotten enough sleep. He felt hyperaware: the rising sun seemed like white fire coming up over the tops of Chelsea's brick buildings, the sunlight spreading on the street like molten gold. The bitter-cold air seeped down his neck and up his jacket sleeves. New York was so much farther south than Nova Scotia, but the temperature seemed more frigid. Maybe that's because Danny was out in it.

Christy said hello to the shopkeepers and delivery people, to the neighborhood residents on their way to work. He said hello to the shy, sad woman—he didn't know her name—but she always wore black. Well, in that way, so did every stylish woman in New York. But this one was different. Christy would see her in her black suits, her black coat, her black jeans and sweater on weekends, and somehow know that she was in mourning.

Behind her silver-rimmed glasses, she had kind eyes. They were dark gray, shining. He remembered that she used to walk past with a man—they'd laugh, hold hands, and some Christmases they'd bought a tree. But the man had been gone for about three years now. Now the woman was alone. She'd stop into the bonnet shop, have tea with Liz, the store owner, and her daughter. The three of them seemed close. Christy was glad of it.

The shy woman acted unfriendly this year—as if she had seen or heard about the fight he'd had with Danny, and about Christy getting arrested. Lots of the neighbors treated him differently. It hurt him—it did. He wanted to stop people as they passed by, tell them what he'd been feeling when he'd wrapped his arms around his son, tried to keep him from wriggling free like a seal trying to escape a fisherman's net. He wanted to tell the Chelsea residents—especially the shy woman—that he'd been torn up inside, half out of his mind, afraid of losing his boy.

But he held the words in, kept his privacy and tried to hold on to his dignity as much as possible in front of the people who'd heard him yelling, saw him wild and turned inside out last Christmas in the moments before Danny had run away, and before the cops had handcuffed Christy and put him in the squad car.

Last night Christy had gone out looking, as he had the night before and as he would until he found his son. Christy had closed up the tree stand at nine o'clock, in time to get inside to see Bridget before she went to bed. The minute he tucked her in and heard her prayers, Christy was off.

Where would Danny be? During the year Christy had been in contact with Officer Rip Collins, the cop who'd arrested him last year. Rip had put him in touch with DHS, the New York City Department of Homeless Services, where he'd found out that half the city's thirty-eight thousand homeless were children. They had no record of Danny in their shelter system. They wouldn't—Christy knew that his son wouldn't go to a shelter.

Christy didn't know where to start. In spite of all the years he'd been selling his trees here, he barely knew New York at all. He came here to do his work, make money, and then go home to Canada as soon as possible.

He tried to get into Danny's mind. Gutting out a living from the land was hard work. Christy had known the burden he was putting on the boy—his own father had done the same to him.

Many nights young Christy had lain in bed, dreaming of a life in Halifax or Fredericton, an easier city life, where friends would be many, and girls would abound, and you didn't live or die by whether the nor'easter hit head-on or ten miles to the south.

"I'm going to go to university, Pa," Danny had said the last day of seventh grade, when he'd brought home all A's on his report card. "Mr. Burton said I have what it takes."

"Of course you've got what it takes," Mary had said. "You're as bright as they come."

"Universities cost thousands and thousands," Christy said. "More than we'll ever make. Besides, you already know nearly enough to take over from me now. If I died tomorrow—"

"Stop, Pa," Danny had replied. "You know you won't."

And Christy had nodded, proud because his son was brave and accepting of their way of life. But he'd seen the shadow in Danny's eyes.

Maybe Danny had been thinking of the landslide that had nearly washed Christy away the month before, during the harvest. How the torrent of water and mud had slammed him into a dam of boulders and fallen logs. And how Danny had pulled him out.

What kid wouldn't want to escape that life? Christy thought of times when he'd seen his own father pinned by nature—the hurricanes and gales that had blown through, once breaking his father's leg with a falling tree. Christy had thought, what kid wouldn't long to go away to school? And with a boy as bright as Danny, wasn't Christy a miser and a spoiler to not encourage it?

He cringed from the memory of Danny's face in the schoolroom door. The boy had overheard it all: Mrs. Harwood's praise, Christy's response, and how the teacher's reasoning had turned to pleading. Christy knew Danny had heard, and they had never once discussed it.

Christy knew that university would take Danny away from the farm. Not just for the four years of study, but forever. Because Danny would get a taste of what the world had to offer beyond their rocky coastline and green hillside and acres of pine. Halifax, Fredericton, other Canadian cities would beckon—and he would surely follow.

Little had Christy dreamed that the city would be New York.

Christy's first night here this year—two nights ago—he'd taken the subway down to Battery Park. He'd chosen it because it was just about the biggest patch of green on a map of Lower Manhattan, and because it was near the Brooklyn Bridge—Danny's postcard.

Waiting for the subway train, Christy had walked up and down the cold and cavernous platform, peering into the darkness. Could Danny be hiding in a subway tunnel? But then a train came roaring out, and Christy knew the answer was no—not because of the danger or the darkness, but because Danny would have to be outside, where he could feel the air, taste the snow, see whatever stars a person could see in this city's too-bright night sky.

Christy had emerged from the subway at the very tip of Manhattan. The Staten Island Ferry terminal lay just ahead of him, and he felt salt air gusting in his face. New York Harbor was dark and choppy in the winter wind howling off the Atlantic. Ferries ablaze with light plied the waterways. The Statue of Liberty stood just offshore, holding her torch aloft, as if she wanted to light his way to his son. Being so near the sea made Christy feel like home, as it would Danny, and he started his search feeling braced and hopeful.

Battery Park was nearly deserted. The few people he saw walked with their heads down low, against the wind. Christy's cheeks stung as he looked for people huddled on benches, stretched out in the lee of Castle Clinton. No one was there. He circled up to Trinity Church, its gothic spire black against the halogen brightness. An old man wrapped in blankets sat on the steps.

"Good evening," Christy said to him.

"Evening," the man replied.

"I'm looking for someone," Christy said, pulling a photo from his pocket. "My son, Daniel Byrne. He's just turned seventeen, about six two. Have you seen him?"

"Tall," the man said.

"Yes—have you seen him?"

"No," the man said.

"Please, take a closer look—"

But the man just pulled his head into the blankets, like a bear retreating into his cave, and refused to say more. Christy continued on his way.

He covered Wall Street, South Street, the Seaport with its fancy shops and eating establishments, the wharves with old sailing ships tied up, just like up in Lunenburg—use the past to entice money out of tourists, Christy thought. He walked faster, because the only people he saw were well dressed, well fed, straight from fancy meals or preholiday parties in the brightly lit restaurants and boats.

When he hit Fulton Street down to Pier 17 and saw stalls and the cobblestones glistening with fish scales, he knew he had stumbled upon the famous fish market. It was just before midnight, and the selling hadn't really gotten under way. Crates of cod, flounder, halibut, and hake glistened as he rushed past.

Down the street he saw a fire burning in a trash can—and he started to run. Rip Collins had told him about how the homeless built fires under bridges to stay warm. Shadows danced on the massive stanchions, and people clustered around were silhouetted by the flames. As he drew closer, he saw a motley crew— and his heart tore apart to think of Danny being among them.

When he drew near, he saw five men, two of them not much older than Danny. They all looked up at his approach. Their eyes looked untamed and wary—like the wolves that hunted his hillside, constantly hungry—glinting like metal in the firelight. Christy pulled Danny's picture from his pocket. He showed it but didn't want to let any of them touch the photo.

"Have you seen my son?" he asked.

"No, no, no," they all said.

"Are you sure? Could you look again?"

They didn't reply but went back to warming their hands. Christy's stomach dropped; he wasn't sure whether to be glad or relieved that these grimy denizens didn't know his boy. He looked up at the stone towers rising above them. Walking away, he looked back and upward, and saw what he hadn't seen before; he'd been too focused on the fire and the men and the hope of finding Danny.

The tower was the western support of a huge, beautiful bridge. Christy saw the garland of lights stretching across the East River. He noticed the steel cables radiating down from gothic piers and felt his stomach lurch to see the bridge up close—was it possible Danny had bought his postcard at a shop nearby? If Christy returned to the area tomorrow, he might find the person who had sold it to him.

Convinced—more than ever—that he was on the right track,

he ran to a pay phone and dialed the direct line to the Tenth Precinct in Chelsea. Someone answered, and when Christy asked to speak to Rip, he was told he wasn't on duty.

Now, standing on snowy Ninth Avenue the next morning, it was all Christy could do to try to stay by his stand. He wanted only to search the warren of streets downtown, going into souvenir and tourist shops that sold postcards of the Brooklyn Bridge, trying to find someone who'd seen Danny.

Liz walked out of Moonstruck with the shy woman. Christy watched them speak for a moment, then hug and break apart. As Liz approached her shop, he gave her his best cocky three-cornered hard-sell smile. He was all set to foist off a tree on her, for her window—suggesting that she display her hats on it, instead of normal decorations—when a patrol car cruised up and the window rolled down.

"How's it going, Christy? Good to see you back here," Officer Rip Collins said, leaning out the window and giving Liz an appreciative glance that she flirtatiously ignored.

"Same to you," Christy said, forgetting all about selling a tree to Liz, digging into his pocket for the postcard. "Listen, I—"

"The desk sergeant told me you called last night. I'm on days right now—sorry I wasn't there. What's up?"

"I think I've got a clue about Danny," Christy said. "This postcard—" He handed it through the open window, watched Rip read it, turn it over, look at the picture. Christy's heart swelled, just imagining how he'd feel when they found Danny.

"Right," Rip said. "You told me about this over the phone, when you first received it, back in the summer."

"I'm thinking," Christy said. "We've got to check the souvenir shops. Down by the Brooklyn Bridge, you know? I went down there last night, almost by chance, and it came to me then. I'd be down there myself right now, only I've got to put in my time here with the trees—"

"The souvenir shops?" Rip asked. Christy was leaning down to look into the squad car's open window, and he saw Rip's partner trying to hold back a laugh.

"I don't mean to tell you two how to do your job," Christy said, not wanting to offend Rip or his partner. "But my son must have been walking around down there, by the bridge, and come upon a postcard to send us. Look at it now—see, it's of the bridge at night! The lights like stars, is what Danny must've thought. He misses the night skies of home, I'm sure of that. So, will you check the postcard and souvenir stores down by the Brooklyn Bridge? Show his picture to the owners?"

"Christy, they sell postcards of the bridge all over town. You can buy them right here in Chelsea."

Christy froze up.

"It's like if you go to Ireland—you can buy postcards of the Blarney Stone in Dublin, and postcards of Dublin in Galway. That's just how it is. Go inside that pharmacy right there, and you'll find postcards of the Brooklyn Bridge, the Statue of Liberty, Rockefeller Center—even the Bronx Zoo."

Rip's partner laughed.

"But there's a lost kid out there. Y'know? It's not funny!"

"We know that," Rip said, shooting his partner a look.

"I thought," Christy began, then trailed away as the hope leaked out of him.

"Christy, we're still looking for him. But it's hard, in a city with this many people, lots of runaway kids, you know? I'm not going to give up, though."

Numb, Christy nodded as the two cops shook his hand, then rolled up the window and drove away. He stood on the sidewalk, enveloped by the scent of pine. He wished he could walk away, straight into a deep forest. That's what he always did at home, when missing Danny got unbearable.

Where could Danny be? Where did his son go, when the pain of missing home got tough for him? Because it did, Christy was sure. It had to. His son loved nature more than anything. He climbed trees, jumped from limb to limb, imitated birdcalls, hid under bushes at nightfall and watched the "fly out," when owls would leave their nests for a night of hunting. Danny was better at tracking owls than anyone Christy knew.

And weather—Danny craved the wind in his face. He needed to pore over weather charts, tell his father what to expect in terms of high pressure systems, and low fronts, and heat waves, and the jet stream. If only Christy had listened more. If only he had given Danny the respect he'd deserved—helping Christy predict the weather, so they could run the farm better. Danny needed to feel the extremes of Cape Breton heat and cold.

How could a boy like that survive in New York City?

So shaken was he by Rip's report about the postcards, he barely even noticed Liz, the hat lady, standing just outside her shop, keys in hand, watching the whole thing. He just pulled a New York map from his back pocket and started staring at the green—the wooded places in the city, where his son was likely to go.

4

*C*atherine could barely concentrate at work that day. The sheet of paper was burning a hole in her pocket. Every time someone walked into the library, she felt that she was about to commit a criminal act against the Rheinbeck Corporation—again.

The Rheinbecks were one of Manhattan's oldest families, dating back to the days of the Dutch West India Company. Sylvester Rheinbeck, the patriarch, still owned property up the Hudson that one of his ancestors had received as a land grant before Peter Stuyvesant's surrender. His family had gotten wealthy in the banking, oil, and real estate industries, retaining a love for New York City and its people, sponsoring research and programs intended to benefit others and make life easier for everyone.

The Rheinbeck family had always been good to Catherine. She had gone to the College of New Rochelle and majored in English, then gotten a Masters of Library Science from Columbia. While most of her classmates had taken jobs at universities and public libraries, Catherine had been hired by Rheinbeck to oversee the wonderful private library on the fifty-fourth floor.

The day ticked by. With the days getting shorter, the sun set at about four-thirty. She watched it go down behind the towers of Central Park West and the Jersey Palisades beyond, a broth of thin, orange light spreading across the snowy expanse of Central Park, then trickling into darkness. Soon the building would be empty, and she would "open the door."

Her desk was piled high with reference books, and she flagged every page that showed pictures of angels in Manhattan architecture. Sylvester Rheinbeck had instituted the Look-Up Project. He intended to locate every single stone angel, demon, lion, serpent, and winged gryphon in the borough of Manhattan.

Although he liked creatures best, he was also interested in medallions, wreaths, keys, staffs, ships, Celtic crosses, and other symbols and curiosities carved into stone buildings and bridges. He had long intended to compile a guidebook that included architectural details of buildings, silhouettes of birds observable flying over New York City, cloud formations, and star charts of the night sky that he would hand out in city schools and on street corners—so people would get interested in *looking up*.

Sylvester limped into the library just after five o'clock, leaning on his cane. Catherine nearly jumped out of her chair—she had expected him to be gone by now. His face was long and wrinkled, like a basset hound's. He wore tiny gold spectacles on the end of his nose. His suit had been custom made on Savile Row—twenty years ago. It was frayed at the cuffs and elbows. Sylvester considered clothing a waste of time. He was eighty-two years old and realized that time was short. He wanted to pay attention only to what he considered important things.

"What have you found today?" he asked, leaning over Catherine's desk.

"This cherub's head," she said, pointing to a black-and-white photo in one of the books, "located just over the doorway at a stationer's on Madison Avenue."

"Excellent," he said. "Have you ascertained that it is still there? That it hasn't been knocked down by greedy, short-sighted developers like—" He stopped short, but Catherine was sure he'd been about to say "my son."

"Not yet," she said, her heart beating faster as she glanced at the clock—five-twenty.

"Developers want to block the light," he said. "They want to build towers into the sky, covering every inch of blue. My grandfather himself cared not a whit for the shadow this building would cast on Central Park—and the sky it would obliterate."

"You're trying to make up for it, Mr. Rheinbeck," Catherine said. "I know."

"If only my son saw it the same way. My father's ways seem to have skipped a generation. But how are city children supposed to dream, if they can't watch clouds on spring days? If they can't go into the park on cool summer nights and lie on their backs and gaze up at the stars?"

"I don't know," Catherine said, glancing over at the service door.

"People need to look up," he said. "Even in the concrete canyons of New York City. I don't care whether it's bird watching, or angel watching, or sky gazing that gets them to do it. As long as they do it."

"We're making good progress," she said, gesturing at her files, the stacks of books on her desk.

He shook his head. "Time is slipping away," he said. "I'll be dead before we're finished. Catherine, with everything Rheinbeck stands for—the banking divisions, and brokerage departments, and all the energy work we do, and all the buildings my son seems intent upon putting up—nothing makes me prouder than what you're doing here in this office. I just came to say, keep up the good work." Without waiting for a reply, he turned and walked away.

Catherine's eyes filled with tears. She heard his cane clomping all the way to the elevator. She felt guilty for taking advantage of her boss. She had done it all through the last year, and she was about to do it again: this was how she repaid him. To top matters off, unlike Sylvester Rheinbeck, she didn't even believe in her work. Would people really look up, as a result of their project? And would their lives improve if they did?

Making sure the elevator had gone down, she went to the service door. It gave onto an interior staircase, used primarily by the janitor for collecting garbage once a week, on Fridays. Catherine's heart was beating fast. Nearly a year ago she had opened this door for the first time. Now it was a fairly regular thing.

Turning the knob, she pulled the door open.

Danny Byrne stood there, tall and ruddy, wearing a jacket Lizzie had scrounged from the goodwill bin at St. Lucy's. His hair was long, curling over his collar. He was still too young to have to shave every day, but his beard was starting to come in, scruffy in patches. His eyes looked strange, wounded—the expression oddly flat, just as his father's had looked that morning—as if he'd been through more than he could handle.

"Hi, C," he said.

"Lizzie gave me your note," she said. "Mr. Rheinbeck came up just as I was about to open the door."

"I know. I heard him," he said, sounding worried.

"Come here," she said. "Let me give you a hug." She opened her arms as he leaned forward, not wanting to take or give too much affection, needing to maintain the tough exterior he created last Christmas, the day he started to live on the streets. Catherine and Lizzie had watched the whole scene with his father, had seen him scrounging in garbage cans the next day.

They had "adopted" him, deciding they would do their best to mother him—or at least help him out as much as he'd let them. He never liked to talk about his father or sister, or about Nova Scotia. He came and went without any fanfare, disappearing so magically that Lucy had nicknamed him "Harry Houdini," the magician on whom she had done her school report.

During his first months here, he'd refused to stay in Catherine's or Lizzie's home, or at a shelter, or anywhere else they tried to find for him to sleep. It was as if he wanted to punish himself for running out on his father and sister. He had plans here in New York, but he wasn't going to let himself be comfortable while he carried them out.

But then one day he'd asked Lizzie if he could use her address to apply for a library card. She said yes, but he'd need to present an ID. He had flinched at that idea, so she'd told him about Catherine's library. Catherine had invited him after hours to use the books and reference materials, and he'd fallen asleep with his head on the carved mahogany desk.

After that he'd come here many times. Catherine had given him his own blanket, and he would sometimes fall asleep on her window seat, stretched out over the heating vent, facing toward the window with its incredible view of Central Park.

"So you want to sleep here tonight?" she asked.

"That's not why I came," he said.

She stared at him, watching the furrow deepen between his eyes as he thought about what he wanted to say. He looked so young and so old, both at the same time. The scar on his cheek was still raised and red—he'd been knifed one night last winter, sleeping under a bridge in the park. Without insurance or money, he hadn't gone to get stitches—till Catherine saw him. And then she'd taken him to the emergency room at St. Luke's–Roosevelt.

"You know I have my own place now," he said, seeing her stare, wanting to set her mind at ease.

"Where is it?" she asked, because she didn't believe him. One hard fact was that he lied when it served him. He had an agenda about being here in New York, and no one knew what it was—but he wasn't going to let anyone get in the way. Catherine knew he lied to both her and Lizzie to get them off his back.

"I can't tell you that," he said. "It would be like Houdini giving up his magic tricks."

"Oh, Harry," she said, watching his smile broaden. He was seventeen now, but still a boy; he had been thrilled by Lucy's nickname. "Well, if you don't want to sleep here, you must have come to use my books. Just be careful to keep the blinds down, if you have the lights on late. I wouldn't want Sylvester Junior to be heading home from the opera and come up to check."

"Are you afraid you're going to get caught for helping me?"

Catherine looked down. It was hard for her to explain the

combination of things she felt. Although Rheinbeck had a tradition of philanthropy, the company had a strict policy about not allowing outsiders to use the library. Catherine knew that it was because so many of the volumes were rare first editions, collected by family members over the generations. So she felt guilt over letting Danny up here.

"Maybe I shouldn't come here," he said. "I don't want to get you into trouble."

"Don't worry about that. Hey, do you have any new pictures?" she asked.

"No. I was going to tell you—I ran out of film."

Opening her desk drawer, she handed him a new roll. "You know . . . your father and sister are back."

He nodded. "I know. I went to Chelsea last night and saw."

She was silent, waiting.

"There's a favor I wanted to ask you. You don't have to do it. I can probably figure out another way—"

"Ask me," Catherine said, cutting him off. Requesting help seemed to be the hardest thing in the world for him.

He cleared his throat, gazed out the window. From high above, Central Park was wide and dark, streetlamps dotting the landscape. Gapstow Bridge arched over the pond, reflecting a blaze of city light. Skaters circled and twirled on Wollman Rink. He stared down for so long, Catherine wondered whether he had lost his nerve.

"It's about my sister," he said after another long moment. When she looked into his eyes, she saw such intense emotion, it shocked her. His voice was shaking, and she knew he was trying to hold back tears. In all this time, she had never seen Danny like this before.

"You miss her, don't you?" she asked.

He shook his head swiftly. "Don't ask me that," he said.

"Danny, you could stop by the stand. I'd go with you, if you wanted." Although she didn't like the tree man, she felt sorry for him, not knowing where his son was.

"Stop talking about him," he said in a rush, "or I'll leave now. I will."

She smiled tenderly. He made it sound like such a threat, as he had all through the year, when she would suggest that he write his family a letter, or call them, or let her call them for him. He never spoke about them—she didn't know whether his father beat him, or mistreated him, or whether he just hated living on a farm so far north—it must have been difficult and lonely for a boy his age. All she knew was that he had a plan, and he wasn't going to let anyone get in the way of it.

"I'll stop talking about him," she said now.

"Okay, then," he said, taking a deep breath. "You don't have to help me, but if you want to . . . there's something I wondered if you would do on Friday night."

And then he asked her.

Standing at his tree stand, Christy had it all planned. He'd get some Chinese takeout for Bridget—her favorite, sweet-and-sour shrimp—and eat it with her. Then he'd read her a story and hope she fell asleep fast. He didn't want her to feel neglected or left out, but he had to get out on the streets, looking for Danny.

He had made money today—a few people bought trees, and even more took home wreaths. Stamping his feet, he tried to stay warm. Just a few more minutes, and then he could close up for the night. His ears and cheeks stung. He chased away the cold by thinking about where he'd search for his son. Just then he heard footsteps crunching through the snow, and he looked up and saw the shy woman in black hurrying down the street.

"Good evening to you," he said, giving her the old grin.

"Hello," she said—and to his shock, stopped right in front of him. She was about five five, slender in her black coat, her scarf pulled up over her chin. Even at night her gray eyes gleamed behind her fine silver-rimmed glasses. Her wheat-colored hair was straight, shoulder length. He noticed her earrings—tiny moonstones, exactly like the kind that washed up on the beaches of Pleasant Bay.

"Did you want to buy a tree?" he asked.

"No," she said.

"A wreath, then?" For some reason, the hard sell wasn't coming easy to him just now. Maybe he was tired. Or maybe he just wanted to get out on the hunt for Danny. Or maybe it was the way her gray eyes were staring at him, as if taking his measure.

"I wanted to invite your daughter," she said slowly, clearly, "to join me and my friends tomorrow night."

"Bridget? You're asking Bridget along with you and your friends?" he asked, the invitation making him so happy, just making his heart absolutely soar.

"Yes," she said, "to the tree lighting, at Rockefeller Center."

"Oh, that's grand," he said. "She'll be thrilled. That's a dream of hers, to go see that tree lighting. Both hers and her brother's—" He stopped himself. Was it his imagination, or did she flinch? He carried on, just too happy to hold it in. "It's a big Norway spruce, she tells me—an eighty-footer. Saw it on TV and all."

"So you think Bridget would like to join us?"

"I'm positive of it," he said. "She'll put on her party clothes, that's for sure. Her prettiest dress."

She smiled. "It's going to be cold," she said.

He laughed. He was getting overenthused. Mary had always chided him about that. He couldn't hold himself back when he was taken by strong feelings. The idea of Bridget's face, when he told her this . . . He grinned just picturing it.

"Thank you very much," he said. "Bridget will be very happy. That's her name, by the way—oh, you know that—you said it," he said, just babbling like an idiot. "Why shouldn't you know? We've seen each other over the years, often enough. I'm Christopher Byrne. Christy."

"Catherine Tierney," she said, and they shook hands.

"A good Irish name," he said.

"My husband's," she said. "Although I was O'Toole before Brian and I got married."

"He fell for a pretty Irish lass," Christy said.

"We fell for each other," she said. She paused, and he saw that look in her gray eyes that made him think of her as sad, in mourning.

"Did Brian die, then?" Christy asked. God, he didn't know what came over him—the words were out before he could even think. He saw her blink and then look down, overtaken by emotion.

"He did," she said, just positively rocked.

He felt the vibrations pouring off her and wanted to tell her about Mary, about how hard it was to get through the death of a spouse, to let her know that he understood. But for once, his tongue was tied. "I'm sorry" was all he could say.

She nodded; he saw her eyes glittering as she bowed her head. When she looked up, the earlier warmth and light were gone from her—she was guarded again, transformed by the swoon. They made plans for Friday, tomorrow—Bridget would be here at five o'clock. Catherine, Liz, and Lucy would meet her, and they would go see the tree lighting.

They said good-bye. Christy watched her walk away. He cursed himself for upsetting her. She had seemed so much lighter for a moment, as if a little of her grief had been lifted. That's what he wanted to tell her—in fact, the feeling was so strong, he actually left his stand and followed her down the avenue.

He wanted to tell her that it got better. That grief, as paralyzing as it sometimes seemed, got lifted a tiny bit at a time. You hardly noticed. One day you'd be going along, feeling crushed by the weight—and suddenly you'd notice yourself smiling at the sun. Or enjoying the taste of an apple. Sure, you'd go back into the black again—but what Christy wanted to tell Catherine was that once it started lifting, the black was never quite as terrible again. That's how it had been for him, after Mary, he wanted to say.

But as he ran closer, he saw her stop in her tracks when she got to Twentieth Street. Something made him hang back and watch. She stood very still. He saw her draw in a breath. She stared up. He followed her gaze and would have sworn she was focused on a tiny window in one of the pretty brick row houses.

She took one slow step, then another. Christy thought she looked scared, as if she feared the street was haunted. He watched her approach the house, reach for the cast-iron handrail, and pull herself up the brownstone steps. His own heart was pounding, just watching her pause on the top step, as if she didn't want to go inside. Then he saw her use her key in the latch, close the heavy ornamented door behind her.

Christy never got to tell her what he'd wanted to say: that when things seemed worst, she should have the most faith. That attitude had gotten him through losing Mary. . . .

If only it could get him through missing Danny, he thought as he walked over to close up the stand, hurrying to give Bridget the exciting invitation. But this was different. His son was only seventeen, lost to the streets of New York City. The fear and grief crushing Christy about Danny was worse than what he'd felt after losing Mary.

Worse than anything in the world.

5

*O*n *Friday night Lizzie had hats for* everyone. When Catherine walked up to Christy's tree stand, it was already dark out, with all the city lights just starting to twinkle. The air felt like snow—a festive prospect for the tree lighting. Bridget stood beside her father, swarmed by Lizzie and Lucy as they adjusted the green knit hat over her thick red hair.

"We have a white one for you, Catherine," Lucy said, handing it to her.

"Catherine Tierney, I'd like you to meet my daughter, Bridget Byrne," Christy said. Catherine shook Bridget's hand, thinking of how much she resembled her brother, Danny.

"I'm happy to meet you," she said, smiling at Bridget. "I feel as if I know you. I've seen you grow up over the years."

"We all feel that way," Lizzie agreed.

"Thank you for inviting me," Bridget said. Her voice was quiet and shy, but her green eyes were alive and bright.

"She's a good girl," Christy said, looking tired and decidedly less fiery than he had yesterday evening. His weathered face was etched with lines, and he had circles under his eyes, as if he had been up all night. "You don't have to worry about her misbehaving."

Catherine flushed. Was he referring to Danny? She didn't dare look at Christy just then.

"I'll be good, Pa," Bridget assured him.

Just then a tree customer approached, and they all said good-bye. Trooping toward the subway, they looked very festive in Lizzie's hats. Although they were all hand-knit by the same person, each was trimmed differently. Bridget's had a candy cane stitched to the band, Lucy's had a wreath, Lizzie's had a candle, and Catherine's had a plain green Christmas tree.

"Why doesn't Catherine's tree have any lights or ornaments on it?" Lucy asked, peering up at the white hat.

"I don't know," Lizzie said. "The hat artist didn't put any on."

"Some people think trees are more beautiful just bare," Bridget said. "With just pine cones, and salt spray, and sometimes birds' nests or feathers in the branches."

"Really? A Christmas tree with a bird's nest in it?" Lucy asked, a true city girl shocked by such a magical-seeming thing.

"Yes," Bridget said. "It happens all the time in Nova Scotia." Lucy fell into step as Bridget told about how just last Christmas season her brother had found a nest with two unhatched speckled eggs in the middle branches of a blue spruce. Catherine and Lizzie lagged behind.

"What's going on—what did Danny say?" Lizzie whispered.

"He wants us to stand at the rail, just above the skating rink, on the Fiftieth Street side."

"Us and everyone else in New York! He's going to try to find us? What did he say about wanting to see his sister? He's not going to try anything crazy, like kidnapping her, is he?"

"No. He said—"

"Because whatever reasons he has for wanting to be here, and why ever he and his father don't get along, Bridget is only twelve. Much too young for what he's doing."

"He knows that," Catherine said. "I think he's having us do this, not so he can meet her . . . but *for* her."

"For her?"

Catherine nodded. "He told me she's always dreamed of seeing the tree lighting, from the time she was a little girl. She watches it on TV. Their father is always so busy working."

"He wants us to make sure his sister has a special time— that's it?"

"Yes."

"I think we can do that," Lizzie said.

Going to Rockefeller Center was a trip for Lizzie, in more ways than one. The crowds were huge, the shop windows were as meticulously produced as Broadway musicals, people wore fur coats, high heels were the norm, and everyone seemed laden down with at least five bags. The Christmas capitalist spirit was alive and well up here. Although strictly speaking this was midtown Manhattan, the fact that it was north of Twenty-third Street made it uptown to Lizzie.

New Yorkers were, by and large, either uptown or downtown. Some people now claimed that downtown was Canal Street and points south, but Lizzie, as a native New Yorker, knew that that had been invented by realtors. Lizzie knew that downtown was a matter of attitude. Uptown was caring whether a person's purse was Prada or Fendi. It was going to Lincoln Center in a limousine. Uptown hair was always done by someone whose name you recognized. Many uptown apartment houses prohibited pets. Uptown was caring about the difference between Barney's and Bergdorf Goodman. Uptown was spending a lot of money. Uptown was waking up early and checking the stock prices.

Downtown was never waking up early—unless you had a kid in first grade. Downtown was creativity. It was taking for granted the fact that you could have a pet in your apartment. Downtown was sharing an air shaft with the Hotel Chelsea and seeing a flaming mattress flying out the window in the middle of one night. Downtown neighbors were frequently guitarists or people taking guitar lessons. Downtown was hats and tea sets from Chez Liz.

Lizzie was decidedly *downtown*. She claimed that she got nosebleeds if she went above Twenty-third Street. None of her romances with uptown men had ever progressed past the cocktail stage. In fact, the only reason she was doing this tonight— braving Rockefeller Center—was because of Catherine.

They started out at Miss Rumple's for tea, right next door to the Rheinbeck Tower. Lizzie watched Lucy and Bridget peruse the menu, with Catherine helping them choose between tiny sandwiches of ham and cheese or peanut butter and apricot jam, between Darjeeling and wild thyme tea. Catherine was taking Danny at his word, making sure his sister had a wonderful time.

The waitress seemed very haughty, but Catherine took it in

stride—she could easily navigate the uptown shoals. She had, in fact, married an uptown man. Lizzie had been so surprised—at first—when her best friend had introduced her to Brian. He had been a Carnegie Hill kind of guy, with a co-op on Madison and Ninety-first, a membership in the Harvard and Union Clubs. He worked at a Wall Street law firm. Lizzie had briefly considered taking her friend for an exorcism—falling in love with a lawyer, for God's sake.

But Brian had turned out to be a really extraordinary lawyer—and person. He cared completely about the underdog. Although he represented big corporations, he gave time and money to Amnesty International, New York City Audubon, and Community Access. At the time they met, he was volunteering at St. Ignatius Loyola's soup kitchen and mentoring a kid from East Harlem.

His firm represented the Rheinbeck Corporation, and he had spotted Catherine in the elevator. They rode up to the fifty-fourth floor, and she turned to him. "This is the library floor. Perhaps you want one of the offices?"

"No," he'd said. "I want to ask you out to dinner tonight." She'd accepted, and they'd gone to Aureole, the next night Le Bernadin, then Café des Artistes—some of the best restaurants in New York. On the fourth day Catherine had said to Lizzie, "He's wonderful. He really cares, really wants to change the world. But I've never seen him out of his suit! And the places he takes me—they'd be great once a year. But every night..."

"Tell him you need pizza," Lizzie urged. "It'll be a test. If he turns up his nose, you'll know he's just a stuffed shirt."

And so Catherine had. She suggested they go out for pizza—in jeans. And Brian had risen to the occasion, laughing, saying he'd wanted to take her to special places because she was so wonderful and because he'd wanted to impress her; and Catherine had smiled, saying if he really wanted to impress her, he'd take her to John's, down on Bleecker Street. They'd gone and discovered they both liked their pizza plain. . . . It was there, relaxing together, seeing Brian in jeans for the first time, that Catherine had started falling in love.

He learned that Catherine had grown up in Chelsea—not quite poor, but as the daughter of a New York City cop, far from rich. Crossing West Twentieth Street on her way to St. Lucy's School, she would dream of what it would be like to live in one of the beautiful townhouses of Cushman Row—she showed him one night, on a moonlit walk. And when they got married, Brian bought one for her.

Brian had adored Catherine every minute of his life with her. They had had six years together. Melanoma had been a very fast way to die—go to the doctor to have a mole looked at, be dead eight weeks later. Sometimes Liz agreed with her best friend—turning her back on God for taking him from her seemed the only sensible thing to do. Liz had days when her prayers were all about yelling at the Most High. Not just over the loss of Brian but over the loss of Catherine.

Liz couldn't bear to see her friend suffer. These weeks before Christmas, when Brian had passed away, were the worst. Catherine would look for him everywhere. She'd see mist in the air, imagine it was his ghost. Lizzie was quite sure she spent most nights in December haunting the little room up in the roof of their house, which she and Brian had always planned would be their children's nursery.

Catherine had the nursery but no children. And no Brian. That was why, Lizzie knew, she was so emotionally involved with Danny. Brian had cared so much about the homeless and hungry, about kids in trouble, families who couldn't stay together. He always walked around with a pocketful of dollar bills, giving them to panhandlers.

"You can't ask what they do with it," he'd told Catherine. "You can't judge them. If you give them money, and they turn right around and buy a bottle with it—that has to be their choice. People need to hold on to their dignity."

Lizzie knew that that was what Catherine was trying to do with Danny. She had tried to get him to call home and, when he refused, offered him all the help she could—she referred him first to the Family Orchard outreach liaison, and then, without his knowledge, to child welfare.

"He's only sixteen," she had said to Lizzie last year. "They can't force him to go home, but maybe they can convince him to get off the street."

But Danny "Harry" Byrne had outfoxed them every step of the way. He was a country boy from the Canadian seacoast, with a hunter's skills and a tracker's wiles. Whenever child welfare got close, he was gone. Lizzie knew he'd slept a few times in Catherine's office, a few summer nights in Central Park. Other than that, his whereabouts were a mystery.

Catherine had given up trying to figure out Danny's whys-and-wheres. She'd stopped trying to change or control the situation—and adopted Brian's method of giving without asking questions.

It was hard, Lizzie knew. But seeing her friend smiling, leaning over to help Bridget spoon some Devon cream onto her scone, filled Lizzie's heart. Catherine's spirit seemed alive tonight. Her gray eyes were dancing. It made coming uptown a little easier to take.

Bridget held her breath, standing in the sea of people at Rockefeller Center, staring up at the great tree. Beautiful skaters glided around the blue-white ice rink down below—nothing like the bumpy rustic ponds she and Danny used to skate on at home. A band played Christmas carols, and cameras flashed constantly. Rising around the scene were buildings as tall as the sky, every window twinkling with light.

"See that gold statue?" Lucy asked, pointing at the almost naked golden man, presiding over the skating rink. "That's Prometheus. He was the wisest of all the Titans—he gave fire to humans."

"Wow, you know a lot," Bridget said, gazing down at the younger girl. Lucy was just nine—four years younger, the same age difference as between Bridget and Danny.

"We study myths in school. How come you don't go?"

"Go?"

"To school."

"Oh, I do. But we get to come to New York for December so my father can sell his trees. That's how we live."

" 'We'?" Lucy asked, wrinkling her brow.

"My brother," Bridget said.

"Harry!" Lucy said.

"No, his name is Danny," Bridget corrected. She watched Lucy turn as red as her name—the blush spread up her neck, into her cheeks, as she glanced up at her mother and Catherine. "That's okay," Bridget said, because the little girl looked so embarrassed.

"Do you miss him?" Lucy asked.

Bridget nodded. She wondered how much Lucy knew, how much anyone knew, for that matter. She stared up at the massive blue spruce. She could almost see it growing in Nova Scotia, on a hillside at the farm, standing strong against the sea winds blowing from the east.

"So much," Bridget said. "More than anything. Pa, too. He goes out looking for him every night."

"Your father does? Every night?"

Bridget nodded. "I wish my father had come, because Danny's here now," she whispered, under the buzz of the crowd, and the music playing.

"You mean right now?" Lucy asked.

Bridget nodded. "I feel him," she said. "He's—he's looking after the tree. Till the lights go on."

"What happens then?" Lucy asked, spellbound.

"The tree comes back to life . . . in a new way. When the lights are turned on, it fills everyone's heart. Just like, well, it probably sounds weird . . . but just like the way you feel on Christmas morning. The tree—I can't explain it. But the tree wasn't cut down in vain. It was cut for a reason—to make everyone who sees it believe in the season."

"Believe what about the season?" Catherine asked.

Bridget looked up, startled. She hadn't realized that Catherine was listening. She cleared her throat. Explaining this to Lucy was one thing; children understood about such matters naturally, even city girls like Lucy.

"Believe in the goodness of the season," Bridget said, her voice breaking, partly because she felt nervous saying it out loud, and partly because her beliefs in the Christmas season had been tested last year, when Danny ran away.

"It sounds almost magic," Lucy said, staring up at her mother with an oddly dangerous look. "Like *Harry Houdini*."

"Sssh, sweetheart," Lizzie said.

Just then the announcers began to talk, their voices ringing out of loudspeakers. The crowd pressed even closer together, trying to get the best view. Bridget's heart was tapping in her chest—any second now, the lights would go on. She wished she knew where Danny was; and she wished her father could be here right now, to see such a beautiful moment. She missed her mother, who had never even been to New York City.

She felt someone take her hand. It was Catherine. Somehow Catherine had read her mind—there was something about her that made Bridget believe that Catherine understood the magic. Catherine had invited her to come here, to see the tree lighting. She wore black and had sad eyes behind her thin silver-rimmed glasses. Her hand held tightly to Bridget's, as someone in the crowd began a countdown.

"Four—three—two—one!"

And suddenly two things happened: the magnificent tree was ablaze with thousands of lights, and someone pulled Bridget's hat from her head.

"My hat!" she cried out, touching her head.

She wheeled around just in time to see a boy running, dodging through the crowd. He wore a different jacket, and his brown hair was long now, but she knew it was her brother who had stolen her hat. Bridget cried out, "Danny!"

But he was gone. Lucy crouched down beside Bridget, retrieving her hat. Bridget was almost disappointed to get it back—she had liked to think of her brother taking it. But when Lucy handed the green knit back to her, Bridget saw a piece of white paper folded inside. Since Lucy hadn't spotted it, Bridget decided to wait for a moment of privacy. Palming the paper, she raised her eyes to the tree.

Everyone was gazing upward. The lights on the tree were as bright as Nova Scotia stars. Her brother had been here the whole time, standing watch. Bridget had felt it, had *known* he would guard the tree. She wanted to run home and tell her father. Trying to catch her breath, she hoped no one would guess what had just happened.

"Pa," she whispered, before she could help herself.

When she glanced up, expecting to see everyone staring at the brilliant lights, she saw Catherine looking down at her instead. Catherine's eyes were sparkling, as if she had just seen the lights on the tree turn to stars. As if she had suddenly witnessed the spirit of the season.

"Goodness," Bridget whispered, looking into Catherine's eyes.

"Goodness," Catherine whispered back.

6

*C*atherine lay in bed on Saturday morn-ing, the covers pulled up to her chin. Snow was falling, driven by the Hudson winds, tapping against her window. She kept thinking about last night—how, at the minute the tree lights went on, Bridget had whispered, "Pa." She had wanted her father to see . . .

Getting up, Catherine's bare feet were cold on the wooden floor. She padded upstairs to the attic room, where she went every day. Sitting in the rocking chair, she wrapped herself in the afghan and stared out the tiny window. The snow was white, furious, and she hoped Danny was somewhere warm.

Just thinking of him made her uncomfortable. Somehow, trying to help him, she had failed to realize how much his family missed him. He had never told her why he'd run away. She had, at first, assumed that his father was cruel to him. But the one time she had asked him about that, Danny had shaken his head hard and said, "It's not that at *all*."

She had seen him last night, weaving through the crowd like the Artful Dodger; even more, she had seen Bridget's look of rapture, clutching onto the note he'd left her. What had he said to his sister? Catherine wished she knew.

"Tell me what to do, Brian," she said.

She listened, but except for tree branches scratching the windows and heat clanking in the pipes, there was silence. Brian had been so good and smart—he'd always known how to help people. She wanted him to guide her now, help her figure out what would be best. Was she supposed to bring a family back together, or help a boy on the streets stay hidden? She couldn't forget Bridget's eyes sparkling as she'd clutched Danny's note, the tree lights shining as she'd whispered, "Goodness."

She thought back three years, to the night Brian had died. Catherine had cared for him through his short, terrible illness. She had loved her husband and been terribly afraid to lose him.

"Don't be afraid," he had said that night. "We won't lose each other."

"How can you say that? How can you know?" Catherine had asked, paralyzed with fear.

"I just do," Brian had said, lying in bed and looking so thin and pale. But the warmth in his eyes was enormous and seemed to defy any possibility of death. Although his skin was yellow, stretched tightly over his cheekbones, his smile was radiant and pulled Catherine to sit beside him.

"Tell me how," Catherine said, trembling as she held his hand. She wanted to be strong but was failing miserably. Here she was supposed to be taking care of Brian, and he had to reassure her.

"I can't explain it to you, love," Brian said, his voice fading. "But I know it with all my heart. I will never leave you."

"How will I find you? How will I know you're here?"

"You'll just know."

"But how?" Catherine had pressed, feeling frantic as she'd watched her husband's eyelids quiver. A silence fell over the room. Outside snow had started to fall, and it brushed against the windowpanes. His breath began to slow. Catherine saw a tear in the corner of her husband's eye—their time together had been so short, and this was so unfair. They stared at each other without looking away, trying to memorize each other.

"Brian—tell me?"

"Listen for me at Christmas," he had whispered. "I'll say hello to you, every year."

"But how?"

"I believe in goodness, Cath," he'd said. "And what we have is so good. It can't die . . . I refuse to believe it. Don't let it. Keep our love alive, however you can. Keep giving, Cath. As much as you can."

"And you'll come back to me? Somehow? You'll let me know you're here?"

Her husband hadn't replied in words but had sat up straight, and his eyes suddenly became bright and clear. Catherine had had the feeling he wanted to get out of bed. Letting go of his hand, she began to lower the bed rail. When she looked up again, Brian was dead.

He had never come back.

That was the thing that Catherine found so hard to live with. She'd never once heard his voice, seen his face. . . . She'd look at mist and want to see ghosts, she'd listen to the wind and want to hear his whispers.

He haunted her heart—that was all. She came up to this room, where they had hoped their children would play. She prayed to hear him, see him. She had begged God to let her speak to him again. But it hadn't happened.

All Catherine could do was remember Brian's words, and keep giving . . . as much as she could. That was why helping Danny, and now Bridget, mattered so much to her.

She saw the snow was falling harder, calling her outside. Closing her eyes, she sent a kiss to Brian. Then she dropped the blanket and ran downstairs to get dressed for the weather.

"Pa," Bridget said, dressed in her warmest clothes, boots, and the green hat Liz had given her last night. "No one's going to buy a tree today. It's a blizzard!"

"Those are the best days to buy a tree," Christy said into the biting wind. "When you drag it home, take it inside, and have a cozy time putting on the ornaments."

"But Pa, the trees have four inches of snow on them now— with more coming! All the New Yorkers are inside. Just imagine how fun and wonderful and *empty* the hill will be today. We'd have it all to ourselves!"

"I know, sweetheart," Christy said, staring down at her. She wanted him to take her sledding.

It had started last night, when he'd gotten home from his search. She was still awake, sitting up in bed with her green hat on, bouncing with excitement. He'd heard all about the wonderful time she'd had with her new friends—the tea, the scones, the Norway spruce, Catherine holding her hand while they watched the lights go on . . .

"The tree came to life, Pa," she'd said last night. "It really did! The lights looked just like stars in the branches—thousands of tiny constellations. I felt so happy to know it was alive again. And it made me want to . . ." She had paused, bitten her lip, and looked away. Christy knew it wasn't possible, but she looked furtive, almost as if she were telling a lie. "Seeing the tree all lit up put me in the mood to go sledding, Pa. At that place you took us once, remember? The first year we came to New York with you? I don't know where it was, but you do, you remember—right, Pa? We have to go there—to that hill! Tomorrow!"

"Bridget," he'd said, stroking her hair as Mary used to do, wondering why she was so charged up, "go to sleep, now. I'll see you in the morning."

And now it was morning, and they were out at the tree stand with snow coming down so hard, Christy couldn't see across Ninth Avenue, and Bridget was at it again.

"Think of how grand it'll be!" she said, dancing around him. "The hillside will be so thick with snow—the sled will just fly."

Christy looked around. Bridget was right about one thing— the New Yorkers seemed to be staying in today. The street was deserted, except for the plows and sanders and the occasional yellow taxi.

"That hill would take too long to get to. Maybe we could go somewhere closer by," he said, trying to remember whether Battery Park had any kind of rise. He gazed down at her, snowflakes sticking to her pale eyelashes. He'd been neglecting her this week, being so focused on Danny. "Just for an hour or so, till the snow lets up."

"No, Pa," she said, agitated. "Nowhere new. The place we went before. The one where you took me and Danny that first year. We have to go *there*."

"That's all the way up in Central Park," Christy said.

Just then a shadowy shape emerged from the curtain of snow. Christy peered down the block. Stark against the white were her black coat and black boots. When she got close, he saw that her eyes looked positively silver. They glinted behind her glasses with the biggest smile that Christy had ever seen in them. It was directed straight at him, which made his heart twist in his chest.

"Hi, Catherine!" Bridget said.

"Hello Bridget, hi Christy," she said.

"You're a vision," he said, smiling. "Practically the only person we've seen on the street all morning. A reverse angel—all dressed in black. Thank you for showing Bridget such a fine time last night."

"Catherine, do you have on your boots?" Bridget asked, bending down to look. "Good! Come sledding with us, okay? We're going to Central Park."

Catherine hesitated. Christy watched the conflict in her eyes. She was shy and sad; she wore black; she'd passed by his tree stand every morning and evening with barely a hello. Yet last night she had shown his daughter a magical time, and here they were inviting her on a family excursion. Christy found himself holding his breath, wanting her to say yes.

Her eyes danced back and forth between him and Bridget, then up at the sky—as if she could see through the driving snow, past the winter gale, to a place of answers. She blinked, her gray eyes serious and bright.

And then she said yes.

Catherine felt excited, as if she were on an adventure. She hadn't been sledding in over thirty years, since she was a child, when her father would take her to Central Park. The city had a shut-down feeling, with hardly any traffic. The snow softened all sounds, and even the buildings appeared to blend into the sky. But that wasn't the only reason—her pulse raced because she knew that something was about to happen.

They picked up two sleds from the basement of Mrs. Quinn's boardinghouse—old Flexible Flyers that dated back to the days when her sons were young. Catherine had grown up in Chelsea with the Quinn boys; John had been in her class at St. Lucy's. She felt a pang to see Patrick's initials carved into the sled's wood, but she said nothing.

The E train came right away, taking them to the Fifty-first Street station, where they changed to the number six train. Getting off at Seventy-seventh Street, they pulled the sleds, cutting over to a nearly deserted Fifth Avenue, where one lone bus was creeping along and two people were cross-country skiing. When the light changed, Christy grabbed Bridget's hand, and they ran across the avenue into Central Park.

Christy hesitated, trying to get his bearings.

"We were here once, four years ago," he said. "I don't remember which hill it was."

"We have to go to the same one!" Bridget said, sounding panicked.

And Catherine's heart lurched. Suddenly she knew. *The same one* . . . the same one that Danny would remember, too. Catherine felt excited: this was what Danny's note had said. He was bringing his father and Bridget here, to Central Park.

"It had a statue at the top, I remember that," Christy said. "A guy with a funny hat."

"The pilgrim," Catherine said. "Pilgrim Hill." She led the way into the park, around the boat pond. She pointed out the elegant building across Fifth Avenue where Pale Male, the red-tailed hawk, had lived for over ten years, raising more than seventeen chicks. Christy laughed.

"Just imagine a hawk choosing to live here in New York City, when he has the whole countryside just waiting for him . . . when he could fly up to Nova Scotia and have a feast every day."

"He's like Danny," Bridget said, pulling her sled. "He was tired of the wild."

Christy stopped smiling. Catherine saw him frown and draw his shoulders up to his ears. He didn't look angry as much as bewildered. Bereft, she thought, her stomach flipping.

When they reached Pilgrim Hill, they discovered where everyone else in New York had gone: the hillside was covered with people sledding. Christy dragged both sleds up to the top, with Catherine and Bridget running behind.

"Look at these initials, carved into the wood," Bridget said. "JQ and PQ."

"The Quinn brothers," Catherine said.

"Did you know them?" Bridget asked.

"I did, in school. They . . . went their separate ways," Catherine said. Something about her tone of voice made Christy look up.

Their eyes met, and she decided not to talk about the Quinn brothers in front of Bridget. He set up Patrick's sled, preparing to get on with his daughter.

"Hop on," he said, holding the rope.

"Pa!" she laughed. "I'm going myself."

"You don't want me to take you down the first run?"

"I'm too big!"

"Of course you are," he said. "What was I thinking?"

He gave his daughter a running push, then stood back with Catherine to watch her speed down the hill. They stood by the pilgrim statue, beneath the bare trees.

"Seems like just last year I was watching her and her brother play in the snow here," Christy said. "They've grown up so."

Catherine heard him stop himself; he hadn't seen his son in a year now.

"What did you mean," he asked, changing the subject, "when you said the Quinn brothers had gone their separate ways?"

"Well, John still lives in the neighborhood. He has a wife and three kids, took over his father's hardware store." Christy nodded that he knew that. "But Patrick joined the Harps, an Irish gang that wanted to be like the Westies—the scourge of Chelsea and Hell's Kitchen. Patrick sold drugs, became a loan shark. He went to jail at Rikers, then got sent to Sing Sing."

"Mrs. Quinn never talks about him," Christy said. "Never a word. I never even knew she had a son named Patrick. She's ashamed of him."

"He broke her heart," Catherine said, and by the way Christy flinched, she could see that his own heart was in tatters. His eyes looked bruised, as if he'd been beaten. Bridget ran up, panting, saying she wanted to go again. They watched her glance around the hillside, as if looking for someone, then jump onto Patrick's sled and take off.

"She's a wonderful girl," she said carefully.

"That she is. She misses her brother something fierce."

And he misses her, Catherine wanted to say. Instead she said, "Is it hard for you to be in New York?"

"In general?" he asked, looking down at her with clear blue eyes. "Or just since Danny ran away?"

"Both, I suppose," she said.

"I used to hate coming," he said. "Back when Mary, my wife, was still alive, I'd dread the month of December. Leaving the family, leaving Nova Scotia. Coming down here, to this place. All the big buildings and taxicabs and honking horns. People hurrying to make money. Including myself, selling my trees."

"You don't think that anymore?"

He shrugged. "I like Chelsea," he said. "For one month. More than that, it would probably wear me out."

"You look . . . ," she began, staring at the circles under his eyes, "a little worn out now."

"That's Danny," he said. "God, I feel I'll go mad if I don't find him. I go looking every night. Under bridges, in parks, down alleyways. The police haven't seen him, the child welfare people haven't seen him." His voice caught, and he blinked the snow out of his eyes. "At least Mrs. Quinn knows her son's in prison. I only received the one card from Danny. I don't even know if he's still alive."

"Oh, but he is!" Catherine blurted out.

Christy gave her a sharp look, stepped closer, and took her arm. "How do you know that?"

Her mouth dropped open. She wanted to tell him everything—that she had seen Danny just last night. The words
caught—how could she betray the boy? But she couldn't stand
the look in his father's eyes. They were face to face; she could feel
his warm breath on her skin, and she couldn't look away from his
gaze.

Just then Bridget dragged her sled up the hill. This time she
was looking wildly around, turning her head from side to side.

"What's wrong, Bridget?" Christy asked, dropping Catherine's
arm.

"Just . . . I don't know," she said. "I thought, I thought . . ."

"Are you cold already?" he asked. "Do you want to go home?"

She shook her head. "No. I want to take another run." Climbing onto her sled, she pointed down the hill.

Catherine's heart had slowed a little, but it was still pounding.
She licked her lips, knowing that when Christy asked her again,
how she knew, she would tell him. But he didn't ask. He touched
her arm again, this time very gently.

"I know that Danny is alive," he said, answering his own question, "because he has to be. My boy has to be alive, and I know he
is. I can feel it in my bones. In my blood. If Danny were dead, I
would know."

"You'd just feel it," Catherine said, closing her eyes, weaving in
the wind as if she were a small tree, "when someone you love
has died."

"Your husband," she heard Christy say. Her eyes were
squeezed tight, but she felt his fingers on her cheek, and she
nodded.

"I know what it is to lose the one you're married to," he said. "A
part of your heart dies with them. You can't quite believe you

can go on breathing. Or that your heart will keep beating. It seems almost unnatural that it does."

"I'm sorry you know that," Catherine said. She opened her eyes then, and she saw his blue eyes looking so deeply into hers that she felt color rise into her cheeks. "And I'm sorry about Danny. He . . ." she began.

Just then a gust of wind shook the trees on the hill. It knocked snow off the branches, sent it tumbling down. The wind dislodged thousands of tiny icicles, making them ring like silver bells.

"I think we need a sleigh ride," Christy said. "Did you hear those bells?"

"They were icicles," Catherine said. "I have to tell you something."

"You New Yorkers are too literal," he laughed. "If there's one thing a lifetime of raising Christmas trees will do for you, it's to make you appreciate hearing magical sleigh bells on a snowy hillside. Come on."

Christy slung the second sled down on the snow. He wrapped one arm around Catherine, easing her down onto the wood. She felt him climb on behind her, his legs around her hips, reaching forward to get her feet positioned on the crossbar. His chest pressed into her back, making her spine tingle.

"You ready?" he asked, his mouth against her ear.

"I am," she said, surprising herself.

"Okay, then," he said.

She felt him push off with one hand, holding on to her with the other. The sled inched through the deep snow till they hit the packed part. They gained momentum, hit the crest of the hill, and started to fly. The sled's metal runners crunched underneath, falling snow stung her cheeks and hit her glasses, the wind filled her lungs. Catherine cried out—the shock of joy. Christy's arms encircled her from behind, and he just held on tighter.

Bridget was trudging back uphill after her third run, when she saw her father and Catherine go zooming by. The sight of her father grinning, as he hadn't in a year, gave her a momentary jolt of happiness. But immediately she went back to despair. Here she had followed Danny's directions to a T, had gotten her father to actually miss a day of work and take her to the appointed spot—and no Danny.

She leaned against the pilgrim statue, hyperventilating from exertion. If she wasn't so frantic to see her brother, she'd be furious at him right now. The snowstorm was blinding, but she peered through it at all the families: parents and kids, brothers and sisters. Tears popped into her eyes.

"Your eyelids will freeze," the voice said.

Bridget whipped around—there was Danny, hiding behind the statue's pedestal.

"You're here! Just like you said in your note," she said, flinging herself into his arms, making the tears gush even more.

"Stop it, stop it," he said. But he didn't push her away. In fact, he held on very tightly. They clung to each other for a whole minute—her eyes were closed, her cheek against his jacket, and she gulped hot sobs as she smelled his familiar smell.

"I'm so glad to see you."

"You, too, Bridey."

"Pa's on the hill," Bridget said when he finally drew back. She scanned the people sledding.

"I know. With Catherine. That's why I have to talk fast—"

"You have to see him, Danny," Bridget said, feeling the panic again, not quite stopping to wonder how he knew Catherine's name. "He's looking for you, every night, after work. This is making him old—it really is. You've given him gray hair and wrinkles!"

"He had those before," Danny said, but he sounded doubtful.

"Not like this. He's . . . aching, Danny. You made him cry."

"Pa doesn't cry."

Bridget clamped her lips tight. If she got started on what this last year had been like, she might start shrieking. And she knew Danny would run away again. So she just stood very still, waiting for him to speak.

"Look," he said, "I'm on a mission, Bridey. That's what I'm thinking this is. I have something I have to do. If Pa sees me here, he'll try to stop me, get me back to the farm." He paused. "How is the farm?"

"The farm's the way it always is! But a *mission*—like what?" Bridget liked the sound of this. It sounded noble, like missionaries going to villages filled with poverty and ignorance, bringing food and schoolbooks. Or maybe Danny was carrying the message of prayer into the sinful city. But that just made Bridget laugh—at the picture of her sinful brother sneaking cigarettes and beer, skipping church, telling her his favorite prayer of a long winter was "Good God, get me the hell off this island." But she knew he was only kidding. Nova Scotia was in his blood, as it was in hers.

"I can't tell you," he said. "Not yet. Not till it happens."

"But in the meantime, Pa . . . why did you have me bring him here, sledding, if you weren't going to talk to him?"

Danny stared down the hill. Bridget followed his gaze, saw

their father and Catherine at the end of a long run—they'd made it almost all the way to the boat pond. Through the snow, they looked hazy from this distance, but Bridget saw her father's height and broad shoulders, and Catherine's black coat, and knew it was them.

She looked up at her brother. His face was thin and sharp, as if he hadn't had enough to eat this year. His brown hair curled over his collar, and his chin was covered with a scruffy beard. Bridget wanted to tease him about it, but then she spotted the tears in his eyes. He had wanted her to bring their father here, because it was the only way he could get close enough to really see him. Danny missed him.

"Now who's the one whose eyelids are going to freeze?" she asked quietly.

He shrugged. Then he kissed the top of her head and pulled the green hat down over her eyes. When Bridget yanked it up, her brother was gone.

7

J *have to tell him,"* Catherine said. "I know I do."

"Now slow down. Let's think about this," Lizzie said.

Late Sunday afternoon they were sitting on the rug in front of the fireplace at Catherine's house, the Sunday *Times* spread out all around them. Yesterday's snow had stuck, and the seminary grounds across the street were covered in white. Lucy and Bridget were upstairs in the music room, trying to play the piano.

"I love that," Catherine said. "Hearing them up there. This is such a big house for one person. It needs kids."

"You wanted Danny to stay here."

"I know. I wish he would now. It would

make telling his father so much easier. If only I could tell Christy that Danny has a roof over his head, that he's safe."

"You're seriously planning to do this?"

"I have to, Lizzie. It was one thing to start off helping Danny. I didn't really know his family then; they seemed, I don't know, almost abstract."

Lizzie nodded.

"The thing is, now I've spent time with Christy. He's suffering so much. How would you feel if you didn't know where Lucy was?" Catherine asked, her gaze boring into Lizzie—knowing the question would pierce her.

"Okay, okay, I hear what you're saying," Lizzie said, shivering at the dreadful thought. "But what about Danny? He's the one I'm worried about. If you betray him, he'll really disappear. At least this way we get to keep an eye on him. He comes to the soup kitchen, and we give him clothes, and he lets you slip him money..."

"And he uses my library," Catherine said quietly, wishing the whole issue were simpler. Lizzie had a good point. She wondered what it said about a runaway boy that his greatest request was to be allowed access to books.

"Do you have *any* idea what he's doing there?" Lizzie asked. "Studying for his GED? Writing a thesis about life on the streets?"

"I..." Catherine began, but trailed off. She did have an idea. The last time he'd visited her library, just four nights ago, he had left two books unshelved. Perhaps he'd been overtired, or excited about his family being back in town—he didn't usually make mistakes like that. Catherine wanted to tell Lizzie, but this was one secret of Danny's she *would* keep. "I don't know," she finished.

Lizzie lay on the rug, a skeptical look in her golden brown eyes. "Mnnn," she said, raising one eyebrow. "So. What are you going to do? Are you going to blow the whistle on him?"

"I'm trying to decide."

"How was sledding with the tree man, by the way?" Lizzie asked.

Catherine stared into the firelight. She remembered the feeling of Christy's arms around her as they'd hurtled down the hill. They'd felt so strong, but somehow tender, as if he wanted to protect her.

"I had a good time," she said quietly. Inside, she felt turmoil. She had had so much fun. Christy's muscular arms had felt so good, just to have that human closeness. She had laughed in the snow—and had so much fun. How was it possible? This was the time of year when she'd lost Brian.

"Are you going to talk to him?" Lizzie asked.

"Brian?" Catherine asked.

Lizzie's expression was steady, a bit impatient. "Christy."

Catherine sighed. She could at least tell Christy that Danny was alive. She wouldn't have to reveal anything she knew about the boy's whereabouts. "I keep asking myself, what would Brian do? It's Christmastime—he's always closest to me now. I want him to tell me—"

"Catherine," Lizzie said, grabbing her friend's hands, shaking them gently. Her eyes were beseeching. "Brian . . . we loved Brian, we all did. But he's gone, darling. He's not coming back to tell you what to do . . ."

"Stop! Don't say that, Lizzie. You don't know what he said to me. He promised—"

"It's been three years," Lizzie said. "I love you so much, and every December . . . I watch you go away. This is the first time since Brian died that I've seen you return to life, have a little fun. The sparkle's come back to your eyes, just a little. I want to see more of it, Cath."

"But Brian's ghost—"

"Catherine, Brian isn't the ghost in this house. You are!"

Catherine bit her lip, feeling as if her best friend had just slapped her across the face. Her whole body was shaking, and she couldn't look Lizzie in the eye. Upstairs the girls were laughing, playing "Jingle Bells" on the piano.

"You're really struggling with this," Lizzie said, pushing herself up. "I don't have to be at St. Lucy's for a couple of hours. Why don't I take the girls to the diner, so you can think about it?"

"That's a good idea," Catherine said, shocked by how much she wanted Lizzie out of her house.

Lizzie pushed herself up from the floor, going to the foot of the staircase to call Lucy and Bridget. They came running down, and Catherine heard Lizzie ask them if they wanted to go out. All excited, they went to get their coats.

"Aren't you coming with us?" Bridget asked, looking up at Catherine with wide eyes.

"No," she said, trying to smile. "I have something I have to do."

"Does it have to do with . . . ," Bridget asked, but she left the sentence unfinished, the unspoken name shimmering between them. Catherine gazed into her eyes—they were filled with un-bridled hope, love, anxiety. "I love them so much," Bridget said.

"My father and my brother. Why can't they talk to each other? I don't understand why it has to be this way."

"Why does it?" Lucy asked. "I can talk to my mom."

"It's different up on the farm. My pa gets up so early. Out the door before the sun is up. And then, when he gets home, he has to fix dinner for us. We talk about stuff...school, the trees. Danny used to pull out his charts and show us where the next storm was—you know, way up in the Arctic, or picking up steam over the North Atlantic. I liked that, because it always warned Pa of what was coming."

"That sounds important," Catherine said.

"It was," Bridget said, sounding wistful.

"But I still don't get it," Lucy said stubbornly, "why your brother couldn't tell your father he wanted to stay in New York."

Bridget shook her head. "Danny used to say we had to solve our problems on our own, not bother him. I just wish that Danny could have talked to him about something besides the weather. I just wish my family could be together again."

"Just keep loving them both," Catherine said, with Lizzie and Lucy hovering beside them. The words felt so inadequate. She wanted to hug the girl, tell her that everything would work out, that her family would be together. But knew that once people broke apart—however it happened—sometimes the closeness they'd had was gone for good.

Catherine leaned close as Lizzie kissed her cheek, their words already blown over. Then Lizzie and Lucy bundled Bridget off, closing the door behind them. Alone in the hallway, Catherine sat down on the stairs. Shivering, she wrapped her arms around herself. Her house felt cold and empty, just like a tomb. Lizzie was right—there was no life here. Three years without any sign, and Catherine was still waiting. Christy was selling his trees just a few blocks north—all she had to do was put on her coat and go see him. She owed him the truth.

But she couldn't do it. Maybe she was wrong to have gotten so involved. Her heart felt so heavy; something deep inside was propelling her up the stairs, four flights to the attic room. She knew how cold it would be up there, and how lonely. But she wasn't ready to leave it, not yet.

Not ever.

Over the next few days the tree business really picked up. It always did, the deeper everyone got into December. Snow fell, and every night the plows would rattle by, fire-breathing dragons with sparks flying as they scraped the snowy streets. That got people in the mood for Christmas, and they lined up at Christy's stand.

They pointed out the trees they wanted to see, and he'd cut the twine that bound them, shake out the branches to give them some fullness. He did it to one white spruce, and a saw-whet owl flew off into the night. The tiny fist-sized predator had been trapped inside the tree, traveled all the way down from Nova Scotia. Christy watched it fly, wished Danny could be there to see it.

The people would pay their money and cart their Christmas trees home. With every transaction, Christy found himself looking up and down the street—watching for Danny, he told himself.

And he was . . . but he was also waiting for Catherine to come by.

He hadn't seen her in several days. And they hadn't talked since they'd gone sledding in Central Park. For a day or so after that, she had walked by, waving, with her great, warm smile— sending a jolt straight through him. What was that for? He'd feel it every time, an electric shock pulsing over his skin. He remembered how his body had curved over her on the sled, his arms had gone around her; how she had leaned back, pressing into him, her hair tickling his face. The feelings were so surprising—and all it took was her smile to bring them on.

Then suddenly he didn't see her at all. Was she sick? Had she changed her route?

At night Christy went out wandering. Funny, but he always seemed to start on the seminary block—West Twentieth, the street he'd seen Catherine turn down that night a couple of weeks earlier. It was always late by the time he got his nightly start—closing up shop, getting Bridget down and all.

This centered him, beginning his night's journey on Catherine's block. He'd breathe in the cold air, let the day's tensions slip out of him. He felt her presence, as surely as if she'd come out to stand on the step. It comforted him, just knowing she was there, nearby.

All the houses looked so cozy. Smoke drifted from their chimneys. Christy was a country man, but when he walked down her block, he could almost understand the draw of the city. He could imagine families living in the townhouses, playing in the small playground across the street on the seminary grounds.

Tonight, crossing Catherine's block, he felt very tired. He had a long night ahead of him; the more he searched for Danny and didn't find him, the more discouraged he felt. Days were slipping by without Danny.

When he got to the middle of the block, he felt a gust of wind. It blew off the Hudson River so hard, it stopped him in his tracks. Christy leaned forward, head into the howling wind, trying to stand upright. Branches shook and rattled; a slate shingle blew off a roof and shattered at his feet.

Suddenly the wind stopped blowing, but the temperature had dropped several degrees. It felt close to zero. Christy looked up at that moment, at Catherine's brick house directly across the street, completely dark except for that one window on the top floor.

She was framed by the small panes of glass. All he could see was her face; she must have heard the wind, come to stand by the window and look out. Christy put up his hand to wave but stopped himself. She was looking way off—far beyond the street. He sensed terrible yearning, a desire for something she couldn't have.

He felt the same longing in himself—he couldn't put it into words. Staring up at Catherine, he felt shaken by a force even stronger than the north wind. He just stood there, riveted for a few minutes, unable to move. But the night was long, and he had a whole city to search. Dead ahead, the abandoned elevated railroad was silhouetted by streetlight—old iron bones, he thought, feeling spooked.

He forced himself to continue on.

At work, Catherine found it almost impossible to focus. She was dying to see Danny so she could convince him to do the right thing—and talk to his father. For several days she had avoided Christy entirely, going around the block to bypass his stand. Now

Mr. Rheinbeck stood at her desk, perusing her most recent additions to the Look-Up list.

"This is charming," he said, tapping his finger on a black-and-white photo of two stone bells. "Where did you find them?"

"Um . . . ," Catherine said, turning red.

"I like bells," he said. "Bells are symbolic. They call people to devotion, to celebrations . . . They are powerful—tools of the spirit! When marauders have attacked places of worship, they always destroy the bells. Because bells ring out the good news— you see? This image is superb. Perfect for our Look-Up Project. Where in the city are they located?"

Catherine pretended to look through her notes. Meanwhile her mind was racing. Danny had found them. One of the ways she gave him money was to "hire" him—to be on the lookout for gargoyles, angels, stone carvings. She had given him a camera to use, and he had delivered this picture several weeks earlier.

"I can't remember, Mr. Rheinbeck. I'd better search my files."

"A church, perhaps?" he asked, using Catherine's magnifying glass to examine the picture. "Very intriguing. Could be liturgical. See this band around the rim of the bell on the left? Those are words, and they look to be Latin."

Just then Mr. Rheinbeck's son—Sylvester Jr.—walked into the library. He had the eyes and bearing of a tiger shark—sleek, economical, and always ready for the kill. Among the company it was well known that Sylvester Jr. disliked his father's projects. He saw the earth strictly as something to build upon, the sky as space to be filled. Money was to be made, saved, and invested—not spent on ridiculous programs to help city residents become dreamers.

"Hello Ms. Tierney, hello Father," he said.

"Look at these bells, my boy," old Mr. Rheinbeck said, passing his son the glass.

Sylvester Jr. just laid it down, staring at Catherine instead. "I was passing by the tower on my way home from *The Nutcracker* last week," he said, "and I saw the library lights on."

"And how was *The Nutcracker*?" Mr. Rheinbeck asked. "I remember so well, the first time your mother took you to see it. She was all agog."

Catherine was nervous, but she couldn't help registering Sylvester Jr.'s facial tic—he recoiled from the memory—and she wondered whether it had to do with the fact that it included only his mother. The world of big business had kept his father away.

"Petronia Boulanger danced the Sugarplum Fairy," Sylvester Jr. said. "She and her husband have put in a bid for the penthouse in our Sutton Place tower. She gave me tickets. What was I supposed to do—decline? Hardly a good PR move. They were good seats, though. *House* seats. Now, about—"

"Sylvester, you could consider enjoying yourself now and then. Not everything has to be public relations. The ballet is meant to enlighten and enliven, to awaken joy! Isn't that right, Catherine?"

"Absolutely. I was just remembering how my father took me to see *The Nutcracker* for the first time," she said, relieved to be off the hook.

"Father, I don't think we need to drag Catherine into a discourse about the ballet. Now, about those lights," Sylvester Jr. said harshly, with obvious discomfort, fixing Catherine with a probing gaze that excluded his father.

"I must have been working late," she said, her heart flipping, wanting to cover herself but also feeling sorry to see another father and son have trouble connecting. She'd been watching these two for years.

He shook his head. "I had my driver stop, and I checked the security log. You had signed out."

"I'm sorry," she said, her cheeks burning. Security had gotten so tight during recent years. She knew that she was skating on thin ice. "I must have left the lights on by mistake."

"There was no one else up here?" Sylvester Jr. asked, peering darkly.

"Who would be using the library at night?" Catherine asked, skirting the lie.

"Marvelous image," the old man interrupted, thrusting the picture into his son's hand. "This really epitomizes what we're trying to do for this city, doesn't it? Ring out the news that life is short, and that we waste too much of it rushing around. Refresh your memory on where these bells are located, Catherine. I want to see them in person."

The two Rheinbeck men, father and son, left the library. Catherine was sweating. She had the oddest feeling that Sylvester Sr. had saved her on purpose. Did he know something? She thought of the practice essay she'd found crumpled up next to those meteorology books Danny had left on the table last week. Catherine had left them there, intending to shelve them. Old Mr. Rheinbeck had walked right over to them on his morning visit that day, tapped them with his long finger, and said, "It takes a smart boy to know that answers are in the sky!"

She shivered, unable to make sense of any of it. She just prayed that Danny would show up soon—she couldn't bear to think of Christy going through another day without news.

8

*D*anny *stood at the corner of Twenty-*third and Ninth Avenue, pretending to wait for a bus. He wore a hat Lizzie had once given him, a derby. "For the mysterious Danny 'Harry Houdini' Byrne," she'd said, adding that it reminded her of a painting by Magritte—of a man standing still before clouds, wearing a derby, his face completely obscured by a huge green apple. Secretly watching his father, Danny was hiding now. He thought the hat helped.

His father was working hard. Although it was freezing cold, with light snow falling and four more inches before midnight, fifty-eight percent humidity, his father was sweating— Danny could see the sheen on his face. Showing trees to people, sawing off the lower branches, wrapping the trees up, hoisting them onto carts or the tops of cars. Danny should be there helping. That's what his father wanted him to do. Danny did want to help. Just...not in the way his father had planned.

Growing up in Nova Scotia, Danny's future had seemed obvious: he would take over the tree business, live on the same island peninsula where he'd grown up. Cape Breton was rugged, and life was dictated by the elements. Tree farmers learned to keep an eye on the sky—prepare for gales, nor'easters, hurricanes, blizzards, droughts. One dry summer could compromise a decade's work.

Danny went to school, but the farm always came first. Two Junes ago lightning had struck a big pine, and the whole grove had gone up in flames. Danny had seen the smoke from his school bus stop, turned around, and run to help his father and the fire squad instead. It had taken all day for them to put out the fire; Danny missed two final exams. Although he'd had all vacation to make them up, summer was the farm's busiest time.

His father thought the fire was out—and that one was. But Danny stayed up late one night, fooling around with an almanac and some printouts from the Canada Centre for Remote Sensing at Natural Resources Canada. He played around with some fire-detection algorithms, combined them with the almanac's plain wisdom, and predicted to his father that this would be the driest summer in fifteen years—with the highest wildfire danger.

And it was. No rain fell in July. His father had needed help irrigating the trees and putting out brushfires. They were on duty day and night, so Danny never managed to make up the exams. He failed the two classes. And Danny saw each failure as a nail in the coffin of his dream. He wouldn't tell his father directly, but life on the farm was killing a part of his spirit.

His father was aware, though—and Danny knew it. It was unspoken between them. Last year Mrs. Harwood, Danny's homeroom teacher, had called his father in for a conference. Danny had felt so nervous—it was after the forest fire, and he thought maybe they were going to kick him out for bad grades, or skipping class—that he'd hung around outside the classroom, trying to overhear.

"Your son is an excellent student," she had said. "He tests in the highest percentiles, and he works very hard in his classes. He's particularly strong in science. His project on cold fronts was so innovative, we featured it in the school paper."

"I know that," his father had said. "I'm proud of him."

"We need to think about his future," Mrs. Harwood had said.

"His future is running the farm."

"That may be. But what about university? He's already missed some critical tests and papers. He can make them up, but he needs to be more careful, moving forward. We'd like him to apply to McGill. We think he has a good chance of earning a scholarship, and—"

Danny's heart had skipped—missed beats, soaring for joy—as he heard those words. But less than a second later his father's words had halted his happiness with a cold dose of reality.

"He's not going to McGill, or anywhere else. I know he's smart—he could get in anywhere he set his mind to. But we run a small farm. I can't spare him for a whole day, never mind four years. Do you understand?"

"No, Mr. Byrne. I don't. And more to the point, I don't think *you* understand. How do you think Danny will feel—maybe not right away, but in years to come—when he realizes you've held him back? He has a wonderful mind and spirit, and he deserves this chance."

At that moment his father had happened to glance at the

door—and he saw Danny looking in. Their eyes met—his father's were burning bright with the anger and shame of having a teacher talk to him that way. Danny half wanted to run in, defend his father to Mrs. Harwood. But he held back. His teacher's words were ringing in his ears. Danny *wanted* that chance.

They'd stared at each other for a few long seconds—and then his father had looked away. Danny had kept waiting for his father to bring it up, the conversation with Mrs. Harwood, but he never did. And now it felt to Danny like a deep cut that had scabbed over. His father didn't seem to realize that Danny had started living for that one month a year when the family would go to New York.

Danny hadn't counted on falling in love.

Not with a girl—this was before Penelope—but with the city lights and everything they stood for, the hope and promises he knew they could deliver. New York City was a place for dreams.

Four years ago he had come down to Manhattan with his father and sister, not knowing what to expect. His mother had always made New York sound like a place where people lost their hearts and souls. "People's heads get turned down there," she'd say. "They're so busy going for the gold ring, they forget to just ride the merry-go-round. They forget to look for the beauty."

To Danny's amazement, he had found the beauty *in* New York. He'd loved it from that first year: taking the subway underground, coming up in a park, or next to a planetarium, or all the way to the end of the line—to a boardwalk by the Atlantic Ocean; walking along one block and being able to choose between a slice of pizza, a fresh bagel, pork fried rice, or a hot dog and a papaya drink; the amazing sight of clouds drifting over the big buildings, throwing their shadows on the walls of windows; beautiful girls smiling at him, making him feel he was king of the world.

In New York, Danny had the feeling he could *be* king of the world. It wasn't like home, where he had to content himself with sunshine, the smell of pine, the sensation of a breeze on his body, and the sound of waves in his ears. As much as he loved those things, he knew he could have them right here—if he went to Central Park, or took a ride on the Staten Island ferry, or rode the A train out to Far Rockaway.

But here in the city he could also have other things as well: if he worked hard, studied right, and didn't get distracted by the beautiful girls he met—Penelope in particular—he could follow his dream, make it come true. Here in New York, it might not matter that he'd failed those two classes, that he wasn't on track to graduate. Danny knew there were other tracks in pursuit of his quest.

Sometimes he'd literally follow clouds. He'd race them through the park, trying to measure their height or wind speed. Were they high-altitude cirrus clouds—thin, wispy, with long curled-up ends? Or were they middle clouds—altocumulus, for example—patchy and scattered, bringing light precipitation? Low clouds were the easiest to chase—big fat cumulus ones, rolling through the sky like laughing babies. Clouds brought the rain that made the trees grow. Danny was learning them all.

His secret hideout—within sight of C's library in the Rheinbeck Tower—was a great place to watch the weather. If only she knew he was here, they could exchange signals! But Danny didn't want to jeopardize anything, involve her in his trickery. No, it was better to be furtive and private, sit up here in his crow's nest and stare out over the sea of trees, observe the systems coming and going. He could block out New York's excitement—study for and pass his GED, fill out applications for the next step in his plan.

Plan, mission, dream: different words for the same thing. Danny might have added *odyssey* and *quest* to the list. This was big, for him. He envied some of the New York kids he met—Penelope, for example. Their lives were so different from his, focused almost completely on education, on their futures; whereas Danny's life on the farm had been all about the here and now. On tilling the earth and planting the saplings, on fertilizing the rows and spraying for pests.

Hard to think about the future, when your back was breaking and the wind was blowing dirt into your eyes. When the sun was beating down and you were so thirsty you thought you'd drop, but you'd forgotten your canteen. When you were spreading fertilizer— literally acres of it—and the stench was making you sick. Hard to dream about the future when you were so mired in the present.

New York kids had it different. Not necessarily better—they didn't have the clean, clear air, or the aurora borealis, or the endless sky. But different. Their parents took it for granted that they would leave home and go to college. Continuing education was assumed, every bit as much a part of life as the sun coming up. Penelope said it was a rare day that she and her parents didn't discuss where she wanted to go to college.

For Danny, it had been the opposite. He hadn't wanted to weigh his father down with his hopes. College cost money. Even more, it would take him away from the farm. Pa was getting older, and Danny knew he was counting on his carrying on. The few times Danny had tried to broach the subject, he'd seen his father's shoulders tighten. The first time had been at the end of a day, when his father was tired from working the field. The second time had been at breakfast, when his father was raring to get out on the hillside.

The third time had been the week before the forest fire. And then the blaze had killed everything. Until Danny got here, to the city, and just decided to stay: make it happen for himself. He'd go back to his father when he'd accomplished his goal—make his father proud. So he stayed here in his hideaway, or up at C's library, working as hard as he could.

The problem was, he got lured down to the street pretty often. The city lights almost seemed to spell out his name. He'd take the camera with him, snap pictures of building ornamentation. He loved to bump through the crowds in Times Square, all those people going to the theater, dressed up in fancy clothes his mother knew only from TV and magazines. He liked to walk up and down the sidewalk in front of the Museum of Natural History, look for the admission badges people exiting dropped on the sidewalk, use them to sneak inside.

Sometimes he'd find two, and he'd call Penelope from the pay phone on the corner, ask her to come meet him. Her family was wealthy, and she'd always offer to pay for him. Danny didn't want that, any more than he wanted to accept public assistance or handouts from Catherine. He would use the found badges to take Penelope inside the museum, stand with her under the blue whale, and whisper in her ear about the whales he'd grown up with, playing in the Cabot Strait.

And now that his family was back in town, he couldn't stay away from Chelsea. He had to see them as much as he could. The problem was, he didn't want to talk to his father: he knew that his pa would lock him down, drag him home to Canada faster than he could say "blue spruce." Danny felt so guilty for abandoning his pa, leaving him all alone to work the farm. So he had to watch from a distance—and pray that Bridey and Catherine wouldn't give him away.

Catherine had been helping him this whole year. She asked very few questions, and Danny liked that. He had the feeling she trusted him, knew that he had to go about things in his own way. She let him use the books in the Rheinbeck Library, so he could study up. She had brought Bridey to Rockefeller Center; that made Danny happier than almost anything, knowing his sister had finally seen the great tree lighting.

Where they came from, Christmas trees meant as much—well, as anything. They were his family's livelihood. Danny's father had always said that their trees brought families together. "Even in bad old New York," he'd say, "where people are always chasing their crazy dreams, piling up money, once a year they bring our trees into their homes and call their families back together."

Danny was proud of that. Even Penelope's apartment, up on the glittering Gold Coast of Fifth Avenue, had a Christmas tree sparkling in its window. Her lawyer father would put his deals aside for one night, staying home to drink eggnog and decorate the tree. She had confided in Danny that the Christmas tree had always been precious to her; because of her father's importance and busy schedule, it was one of the few nights she'd ever been able to count on him being home.

Penelope was the only person he'd ever confided his plans in. He hadn't told his father or sister, Lizzie or Lucy, even Catherine. Just Pen. He remembered the moment still—it was back in September, a beautiful late summer day, standing on the terrace of Belvedere Castle. He'd had his arm around her, pointing out high clouds, veiling the blue sky with a layer as thin as gauze.

"What are they, Danny?" she'd asked.

"Cirrostratus," he said. "They're high clouds, about eighteen thousand feet up, primarily composed of ice crystals. See how they don't have distinct edges? They're good for the trees; they block the brightest sun from scorching the needles."

"It's only September, but you're already thinking about the Christmas trees."

"I always am," he said quietly. "It's why I want to be a meteorologist."

"Dan, Dan, the weather man," she teased.

And he'd just smiled, because in spite of her joking, he knew that this was his life: what he had been put on this earth to do.

Now his father stopped working for a minute. He stretched, looked around. The light was red, no traffic moving down Ninth Avenue. Staring across the street, Danny saw his father spot him. His father leaned forward, peering through the snow. The hat must have thrown him off, but suddenly their eyes met. Danny's heart was pounding. He froze, like a deer caught in headlights.

"Danny!" his father called, coming toward him.

For one minute he wanted his father to catch him—to hold on tight, take him home again. He wanted the chance to explain what he was doing, tell his father that he loved him and was, in a way, doing this for him and the farm. But he didn't trust himself to be articulate enough to put it all in words.

Just then the bus came, and Danny jumped on board. When he did, the hat fell off. His last look, out the back window of the bus, was of his father picking up the black derby in his hands, clutching it to his heart as he tore down Ninth Avenue, yelling after the bus.

His own heart breaking, Danny jumped off at the next stop and did what he did best: disappeared into the city, losing himself down an alley, behind a building, over a fence . . . like a cloud in the sky, like a scrap of mist caught in the branches of a white pine. You might see it, might even think you can grab it, but you'd better not try: it'll just disappear.

That's what clouds do.

And they didn't call him Harry Houdini for nothing.

That night Catherine was late leaving work. She hoped that Danny would show, but he didn't. She took her time walking through the snow to the subway. When she got off the train in Chelsea, she walked slowly down Twenty-third Street. Slower and slower as she got closer to Christy. In contrast to her pace, her heart sped up. At the sight of him, she stopped dead.

"I saw him," Christy said to her.

She spied him holding the hat Lizzie had given Danny, and her stomach dropped.

"How did you get that?" she asked.

"It fell off his head as he ran away from me. He doesn't want to see me. He practically broke his neck running for the bus."

"The bus?" she asked, noticing how strongly he gripped the hat, his fingers digging into the brim, as if for dear life.

"Right over there," Christy said, gesturing through the veil of snow, at the stop across Ninth Avenue.

"Can you come with me?" she asked. When he didn't respond—he seemed so numb, as if in a dream—she slipped one of her hands into one of his and pulled gently.

He followed her, just left his tree stand the way it was, the string of lights twinkling in the cold night air. They made their way down Ninth Avenue, onto Twentieth Street. Her pulse racing, she didn't know what she was going to do or say—she only knew that he was hurting badly, that she had to be with him right now.

Underfoot, the snow was turning icy. Catherine slipped, and Christy caught her. They held on for a minute, standing under a streetlight. His arm was around her; when they started walking again, he didn't let go. Danny's hat was in his other hand.

They climbed her front stairs, and she unlocked the door and turned on lamps. The house was warm, the wood floors gleaming. Christy stood in the front hall, looking around, still holding the derby.

"You can put it down," she said, but he wouldn't let go.

"It's all I have of him," he said.

Catherine shook her head. "That's not true," she said. "You know it's not."

Christy looked down at the hat. "Once when Danny was a baby, he had a fever. It got very bad—nothing we did brought it down. We live far away from the hospital, but I drove him there, him and his mother, as fast as I could. The doctors weren't sure what it was, so they kept him overnight. Mary stayed. When I got back home, I found his teddy bear. I thought . . . I thought I'd never see my son again, that his teddy bear was all I'd have of him."

"And now you feel that way about his hat," Catherine said.

Christy nodded. He couldn't take his eyes off the derby, even when Catherine walked over to him and stood there.

"It's all I have of him," Christy said again, this time his voice breaking.

Catherine gently removed the hat from his hand, laid it carefully on the hall table. He was trembling—she felt him shaking through his heavy brown canvas jacket with its leather collar. Reaching up, she unzipped the jacket, eased it off him slowly. She shook away the snow, hung it in the closet with her coat.

"I want to tell you something," she said.

He gazed at her, his blue eyes blazing with ferocious hopelessness. She knew that feeling, knew it so well. It was as if loss had taken hold of his soul, emptied him from the inside out. Catherine took a step closer, and something made her stand on her tiptoes, put her arms around him. She told herself she wanted to look him straight in the eyes and support him with her strength.

They were heart to heart, and she felt his pounding against her chest. His eyes burned into hers, and the moment was so charged and intense, she nearly gasped. Instead, she touched his face. His skin felt so cold, from being out in the snow all day. She told herself she wanted to warm him up. That's all it was, she thought as she stood on tiptoes to press her lips to his cheek.

Christy kissed her. His lips touched hers—such a soft, gentle kiss. His fingers traced her cheekbones, her throat. His mouth was hot, melting her into his arms. The snow tapped against the windows, orange streetlight slanting through the panes, but Catherine saw stars.

His arms and back so hard under her hands. She couldn't stop touching him, didn't even want to. Christy was strong from swinging his ax, hauling wood, doing hard labor on his farm—she felt all of that as she held him, as he kissed her insistently.

She heard him say, "Catherine." No man had said her name in this house for so long . . .

"Three Christmases," she whispered.

"What?" he asked.

"I haven't, I haven't," she began, still clutching him.

"It's okay," he said, stroking her hair. "Whatever it is."

And she listened to him. She hadn't believed in "okay" for so long. He smelled of pine, snow, and leather. Pressing her face into his neck, she breathed deeply and thought of the north woods. Getting lost in his scent and the feel of his body, she saw nothing but branches and starlight. He felt so solid and real—she never wanted to let go.

"I've hoped," she whispered, "to see my husband's ghost."

"And you haven't?"

She shook her head.

"Maybe that's because you're not supposed to. Maybe you're supposed to stay right here, with your feet right on the ground. You're a living, breathing woman, Catherine Tierney. If you saw your husband's ghost, you might want to fly away with him."

A living, breathing woman. Her mind swirled with images, and her body tingled with feelings: she remembered holding Bridget's hand at Rockefeller Center, hugging Danny in the Rheinbeck Library, sledding down Pilgrim Hill with Christy's arms holding her tight. She'd felt dead, worse than a ghost—earthbound, buried in sorrow. She'd felt like one of Bridget's Christmas trees, cut down, dragged from the forest, but unclaimed and unlit.

Christy kissed her again, in a whole new way, as if he'd just reminded himself that he was a living, breathing man. His lips opened, his mouth and tongue so hot, touching her with a desire that matched her own. This feeling of life had been gone for so long—she felt a long shiver go down her spine. Her skin rippled, the way a cat can seem electric when it's purring.

The moment gripped them, and Catherine opened her eyes to make sure it was real. Christy leaned back, still holding on to her. They smiled at each other. She didn't want to let go of his arms— it would break the spell if she did. Was his heart beating as hard as hers? She pressed her hand to his chest, and he did the same.

"You're giving me a heart attack," he said.

"I don't want to do that," she said, stepping back.

"I want you to," he whispered, kissing her again. His lips were tender, his arms encircling her in a way that made her want him never, never to let go. But then her gaze fell upon Danny's hat, and she made herself speak.

"Christy," she said.

"Catherine."

"There's something I have to tell you."

He nodded, smoothing the hair back from her eyes. She'd had her glasses on the whole time, and he straightened them on her nose. The gesture was so gentle, she couldn't breathe.

"That's right," he said. "You told me you've something to say."

She swallowed, went to the chair, picked up the derby. Glancing inside, she saw the white satin lining—streaked with sand and salt, from where it had fallen off Danny's head—and bright red embroidery. The derby was antique—Lizzie sometimes picked up interesting old hats at the Sixth Avenue flea market—and bore the name of the original hatmaker, Motsch et Fils, Paris.

Catherine handed Christy his son's hat, gesturing for him to look inside. She watched him examine the headband and label.

"It's a French hat," he said. "I was surprised to see Danny wearing something so stylish. It made me not recognize him at first."

"The embroidery," Catherine said, her lips dry, pointing at the delicate crimson stitching. Her heart was skittering in a whole new way, with such nervousness, she wasn't sure she could speak.

" 'CL,' " he said, reading the red letters, looking up at her with bright blue eyes. She expected his gaze to be filled with confusion, but it wasn't. It was total trust, as if he thought whatever Catherine might tell him was bound to help him in his search for Danny.

"Chez Liz," Catherine said.

Now he looked confused. "I don't understand," he said.

"Lizzie buys old hats at auction and flea markets," she said. "She never removes the original labels, but she always adds her own mark. Red is her shop's signature color, and she always stitches 'CL.' For Chez Liz."

"Danny bought this from your friend Liz?" Christy asked, his expression exploding into joy. "Then maybe she knows something! Perhaps she'll remember him—he's a very tall boy, so intelligent and full of life. Let's call her now!"

"Christy," Catherine said, taking his hands, "she gave it to him."

"But," he said, his eyes clouding, "if she knew it was Danny, surely she'd have told me—or told you, and you'd have let me know . . ."

"He asked us not to," Catherine said quietly.

The house was silent. Looking into Christy's face, she saw all the blood drain out. He was pure white, and she was sure he had stopped breathing. He didn't so much pull his hands away as let them drop, as if gravity had become too much.

"You—"

"I've seen him," she said.

He waited, his eyes suddenly darkening, as if night had just fallen over an icy pond.

"We helped him last year," she said, "after the fight between you. The police took you away, and when you got out and took Bridget home, Danny stayed behind."

"That's what he wanted."

"It was," she said. "He was"—she didn't want to tell him about seeing his son scrounging in the dumpster behind Moore's, the restaurant on the corner—"hungry. We helped him get food."

"Danny was hungry," he said, flinching. He shook his head as if it were too much to bear. "I've never let that happen. I never would. Does he hate me so much that he'd rather go hungry than live with me?" Christy grabbed his coat, pulled it on, tucked the hat under his arm. His eyes were filled with rage and despair. He had one hand on the brass door handle as Catherine grabbed his arm.

"It's not that," she said. "He doesn't hate you."

"He talks to you then? He tells you?"

She shook her head. "No. He hardly talks to me at all. But I know. I'm sure of it, Christy. Listen, please. I want to help."

"Help?" he asked, the word tearing out of his mouth. In that instant she felt his hopelessness return—he had trusted her. "All this time I thought you—"

She listened, waiting.

"I thought you were an angel," he said finally. All warmth drained from his eyes, as if he now believed in angels about as much as she believed in ghosts. He swung open the door; outside the wind howled, and snow kept falling.

"This is the snowiest December in over a hundred years," she said suddenly.

He glanced over his shoulder, as if he thought she was crazy, as if that statement had nothing to do with the pain he was feeling. Catherine didn't tell him that she'd read that statement, written in Danny's hand, in his crumpled-up practice essay.

"It's surely the coldest one," Christy said, staring into Catherine's eyes for one long moment. As if he couldn't help himself, he touched her cheek. "The more so for how warm I felt with you."

Turning up his collar, he walked away and, like his son, disappeared into the snow.

9

*C*hristy started off running. *He tore*
down Ninth Avenue through the snowstorm, his heart cracking like ice on a pond.
The city rose around him, a wilderness of
light. At each corner his country boots
smashed through slush and drifts. People
walked by carrying shopping bags, festive in
the snow. Christy felt blinded by the truth
he'd just heard.

How could he feel so betrayed by a
woman he barely knew? He ran faster, his
lungs searing with every breath. His shoulders and arms ached, his muscles burned
from holding her, and from letting her go.
He'd enveloped her with his arms, his spirit—
he'd felt her need, and he'd wanted to give
her even more. Yet she had stood there,

calmly telling him she'd seen his son, that she had been helping Danny all this time.

When Christy had thought his son was...what? Missing, gone, dead. Couldn't Catherine understand that? A woman in black—his sad friend. She was grieving her life away, trading in her very breath for a chance to see the ghost of her husband. She hid from life; she reached for the past. But tonight...

Christy had thought he'd reached her. Holding her, feeling her beautiful body, wanting to talk to her for the rest of the night—the rest of his time here in New York! That was how he'd felt, caressing her hair, assuring her that she was alive, that she was living and breathing and needed to choose to live. Yes, that was how he'd felt—maybe, obviously he was crazy, but he'd had that wild impulse to grab onto her, love her. For tonight, forever, what was the difference?

He'd thought that they understood each other, accepted the truth that life was short and precious and very, very wild. If it wasn't, how could a young husband die at Christmastime? How could a teenage boy—the light of his father's eye, his sister's heart—just run off into the night, never to be seen again?

Why not grasp the chance, just the very most elusive of chances, to have the love and light that were so hard to find? He and Catherine didn't stand a chance. Christy knew that. She was a grand lady with expensive things and a townhouse that cost more than Christy would make in a lifetime. He was a Canadian tree farmer with hands rougher than sandpaper, with bark and sap under his fingernails. But in that one moment—

He'd seen it in her eyes, he thought. She felt it, too. Catherine O'Toole Tierney, beautiful Chelsea girl, kissing him, Christopher X. Byrne. He'd felt her tremble in his arms, looking up into his eyes with the same tumultuous hope he felt inside. But then she'd told him the truth.

The truth about Danny. Had they laughed at him, Catherine and her friend? Christy knew that didn't matter—that was beside the point. All that counted was that Danny was alive, and that Catherine knew it. Christy should be overjoyed about the first part. The second shouldn't even matter. Not in comparison to Danny's being okay . . .

Passing the Maritime Hotel with its portholes, he saw limos discharging people for a Christmas party. Something made him slow down, watch the people climbing the steps to the wide terrace. New York was a strange place indeed, Christy thought. He'd been selling his trees in Chelsea for so long, he'd watched this place go from a home for old sailors to a shelter for runaway kids to this—a fancy hotel and restaurants.

Was this what Danny wanted? Had his son spent his visits to Manhattan longing for parties and glamour? Had he watched his father selling their trees to the beautiful people—and decided he wanted to live a fancier life himself?

Staring at the people walking up to the party, Christy shrank into the shadows. They were wearing black—black suits, black topcoats, a black velvet cape, glossy black boots. His eyes were glued to them: with all the salt and sand and slush on the streets, those boots were polished to a high shine. Christy imagined the wearer stepping out from under a ritzy apartment awning into the limo, and from there onto the hotel steps. People here never had to get their feet wet.

Was *that* what Danny wanted? Had his life in Nova Scotia been so terrible? Christy thought of the farm, of the boots Danny had always worn. From the time he could walk, he had wanted

Sorels—heavy-duty work boots, just like his father's. Christy would hold Danny on his lap while he laced them up. Christy's mind was full of boots now, Danny's little baby boots, and his ten-year-old boots, and his teenage boots, all caked with mud, manure, pine needles, sap, salt, hay, soot.

He thought of the wildfires. Lightning had struck one tree, and quickly a half acre had gone up in flames. Danny had had to miss school to help out. First one day, then another, then the make-up period for his exams. Christy told himself that Danny was smart enough to catch up with his schoolwork. Then one smoky night that summer, with the fires still smoldering, he'd heard his kids talking, when they thought he wasn't there.

They were out on the porch, watching fireflies flit through the tall grass.

"Will you catch me some?" Bridget had asked her brother.

"I'm too tired, Bridey," he said.

"I want to put all the fireflies in a big jar and throw them into the sea," she said.

"What for?"

"To keep them away from the trees. I don't like fire."

Christy had held back a laugh, so they wouldn't hear. Danny hadn't been able to manage the same control—he'd let out a big whoop. "That's a good one," he'd said. "You can't be my sister and really believe that."

"Something keeps causing the fires!"

"Bridey, fireflies produce a substance called luciferin, and it reacts with oxygen, and that makes them glow. It's a cold light—nothing to worry about."

"Are you sure?"

"Yeah." Danny had chuckled. "I learned it in science."

"Well, what *does* cause the fires?"

"Lightning, heat, drought. I was using the computer at school early this spring, checking out this new sensor aboard the NOAA satellite. See, the forest fire research group has plugged in some cool new smoke detection algorithms into the AVHRR/3 transmitter, and I swear, if I'd been able to access that site, I'd have been able to warn Pa about the fire danger here. There's this mid-infrared channel that I think—"

"Whoa, Danny! What are you talking about?"

Christy had hung back, amazed and impressed. What *was* Danny talking about? All along Christy had taught him that farming required lots of scientific knowledge, but toward one specific end: growing trees. So they could be sold for lots of money. Danny was speaking about science in such a different way, with a passion for learning and discovery.

When Christy was honest with himself, on nights when he couldn't sleep, he admitted, deep down, that he worried he might be holding his son back. How could he ask a boy with a mind like that to make his living with a rake and a saw? The questions made him shake inside right now: in his core he knew that he'd driven his son away.

Across the street the people streaming into the hotel looked chic in their black. Now Christy's mind shifted from Danny to Catherine—his sad, shy girl. She'd been chic, too. But he'd never, not for a moment, thought she was wearing black for anything other than mourning. Tonight she'd told him about Brian.

She had seemed so gentle and sincere. Christy had had the feeling it was costing her a lot to get the words out, to confide in him about wanting to see Brian's ghost. And it had given Christy such a feeling of goodness to be able to hold her and assure her that life would, and should, go on, that her sorrow didn't have to destroy her.

Right now Christy felt that it was destroying him. He didn't understand people. Losing Mary, he'd done his best to raise their children. Dutifully he'd maintained his schedule, coming down here to New York, selling trees to all the wealthy people. He had thought he'd instilled good values in his children. And he thought he had better judgment about friends.

About Catherine.

Just then he noticed a patrol car slowly cruising down the avenue. Christy saw the officers looking his way. One was Rip Collins, and he rolled down the window.

"What's happening, Christy?" he asked.

"Just out for a walk," Christy replied.

"Nice night for it—if you're from Canada," Rip said, grinning.

Christy knew he didn't mean anything rude by the comment, so he tried to smile.

"Still looking for your boy?" Rip asked.

Christy shrugged to hide his feelings. The sight of Danny running to make that bus felt like ice in his heart.

"It's tough, this time of year," Rip said.

Every time of year, Christy wanted to reply. He thought of Catherine, waiting for her husband's ghost. How could a woman who'd do that not understand what Christy was feeling about Danny?

"Yeah," Christy said instead.

"Call it a night," Rip suggested. "You left your tree stand untended, and it's all lit up."

Christy started—was it possible? He'd been so undone by seeing Danny get on the bus, that when Catherine came by, he'd walked away, literally leaving everything. He'd lost his mind, he really had. His cashbox was there!

"Thank you," Christy said to the cop, then turned and hurried up the avenue. When he got to his corner, the snow was coming down so hard, the trees were all but obliterated. The string of white lights was a blur. Christy flew to the spot where he hid his cashbox.

It was gone.

He found the indentation where it had sat in the snow, under the lowest branches of a small white spruce. Sticking his hand in deeper, he thought maybe he'd inadvertently pushed it back. As he groped around, branches and needles scratching his head and neck, he realized that the box wasn't there. When had he emptied it last? With all his worries about Danny, and amid his feelings and seeing stars over Catherine, he'd left it with about a week's take inside.

Seventy dollars for a big blue spruce, eighty dollars for the Fraser and Scotch pines, ninety for the Douglas firs, fifty for the big balsams, forty for the white pines, thirty for the small table-sized trees—he'd lost thousands.

Who knew he hid the box there? No, it couldn't be Danny—it couldn't be. But Christy was always so careful. He'd take the customer's cash, stuff it into his pocket, and transfer it into the box when he was sure no one was looking.

His thoughts were a maelstrom—suddenly he found himself thinking of the Quinn boys. Their sleds, carved with their initials, JQ and PQ. John and Patrick. One brother took the right path, the other took the wrong.

Christy thought of his children. Bridget was home now, just upstairs in the boardinghouse behind him, and Danny was God only knew where. Christy would have sworn on his mother's grave that his children were as good as the day was long. He would have given any odds that his children would turn out right and happy, that in spite of his son's very bright mind, he and Danny would be farming the trees from now until his last day on this earth.

But right now Christy Byrne didn't trust himself about anything. He could never have imagined a year without his son.

He still couldn't.

Losing the money seemed like nothing in comparison. But what if his wonderful, intelligent boy had taken that wrong turn? What if Christy's inability to know what his own son wanted had driven him in a bad direction? Kids stole money for drugs— Christy had heard of it happening, even back home. God, what was Danny doing? Life on the streets had to be hard, terrible. How would Danny get food, shelter? What did he do just to live?

When Christy glanced up and saw Rip's police car coming toward him—he must have driven around the block—Christy felt his stomach clench with shame. The officers stopped and got out of the car. They knew by the look in Christy's eyes that the money was gone. Rip took his pad out, and Christy could do nothing but tell him the truth.

An hour later, after some newspeople had heard the report over the police scanner and come to take pictures—Christy wanting to break their cameras, stunned by the flashes, by the audacity and intrusion—the cops finally left. Christy slogged up the stairs into Mrs. Quinn's boardinghouse.

"What's wrong, Pa?" Bridget asked the instant he walked in. She was curled up on the sofa in Mrs. Quinn's sitting room, Murphy on her lap. Her big green eyes looked alarmed, as if she saw her father's defeat.

"Didn't you look out the window?" he asked, knowing she would have seen him talking to the police. Must've been a slow crime night, because not only had Rip and his partner been there, but three or four other squad cars. Not to mention various news teams and a whole gaggle of neighborhood onlookers.

"No," she said, looking scared. "Why? What's wrong?"

Christy tried to smile but found he couldn't. The sitting room was in the back of the house, facing the courtyard—just as well she hadn't seen. Having his money stolen was the least of it; all the neighbors had been kind, telling him they were sorry, offering to buy him a meal. The cops had asked him who knew where the money was, and he'd said no one. He wasn't about to mention Danny. Why had he been in Chelsea at all that day, if he wasn't going to say hello? Had he been planning the theft all along? It all felt surreal to Christy. His body still felt electric from holding Catherine. And his mind was a black hole from what she'd told him about Danny.

"Nothing's wrong. It's snowing hard out," he said to Bridget.

"What's that you're holding?" Bridget asked, gesturing at the black derby.

"It's—it's your brother's hat."

"Danny! Did you see him, then?"

Christy nodded. He felt weary, taking his jacket off, hanging it on the peg behind the door. He laid the hat on the top of a book-case. "I saw him."

"Where? What *happened*? What did he say to you?"

"He ran away from me," Christy said. He had to stop speaking for a minute, to get the emotion under control.

Bridget didn't speak, but just stared up at him. Christy wondered why she didn't look more surprised. As he stared at her, two red patches fired her cheeks. Embarrassed, she buried her head in Murphy's fur.

"You've seen him, too?" he asked with disbelief.

"Uhhhhnnnn," she said with her face pressed into the dog's back.

"You, Catherine, and Liz?"

"And Lucy," Bridget said, her face popping up.

"But why?" he asked, sitting down heavily on an old wingback chair. "Why didn't you tell me?"

"Because Danny wouldn't let us."

"Am I an ogre?" Christy asked. He was beyond numb. His hands gripped the chair arms as he stared into his daughter's eyes.

"Don't think that, Pa," she beseeched.

"I must be," he said. "Everyone's afraid to talk to me. My own son—"

"We just don't want to bother you," she said, "when you work so hard."

"I work so hard for the two of you! Don't you know that?"

"That's why Danny doesn't want to add to your burden, Pa."

"Jesus, Bridget. My burden—is that what you think it is?" He pictured Danny running for that bus. And Christy knew it was true—yes, it was. He'd heard that conversation on the porch, his two smart children, and he'd been afraid of what Danny wanted from life: afraid that Danny wanted to leave the farm. And Danny must have sensed his fear.

"He has his plans," Bridget said now.

"What if they—" Christy began, but broke off. What if Danny's plans included stealing the tree money? Maybe not for drugs but to go to school. Maybe it was that . . .

"We have to be patient, Pa. He'll tell us when he's ready."

Christy listened. His daughter sounded so smart and mature, full of reason. But reason was far beyond Christy Byrne at that moment. His world had cracked in half tonight.

"When he's ready?" Christy asked, tasting tears in the corners of his mouth. "Your brother's barely seventeen, Bridget. I can't be patient. Not when it comes to you and Danny."

10

The tabloids both had the same cover story. The *Post*'s headline blared, GRINCH STRIKES CHELSEA! and the *Daily News*'s read, SCROOGED ON NINTH AVE. The photos showed Christy at his tree stand, unconsciously looking away from the cameras—his face craggy in profile, his blue eyes a portrait of lost, hopeless fatherly love. Inset, right at the top, was Danny's last yearbook photo.

Catherine and Lizzie read the stories at Moonstruck. Both papers reported the theft and included summaries of last year's incident—Christy's arrest for assault, Danny's running away, the charges being dismissed. The *Post* had a sidebar about teenage runaways, and the *Daily News* lumped the story of Danny into an ongoing series about the homeless.

"They make him sound horrible," Catherine said, reading about Christy. "As if he beat his son last year, as if he cares only about making money. Listen to this. 'Daniel Byrne, now seventeen, ran away last December twenty-seventh. Routinely taken out of school for the month preceding Christmas, he worked at his father's tree stand on Ninth Avenue in Chelsea. New York City tree salesmen keep long hours, trying to earn a year's income in one month, and neighborhood residents reported seeing the teenager working until midnight some nights.' "

She shook her head, and then Lizzie took over reading. " 'The administration of North Breton High School declined comment. But Jay LeClair, a classmate of Daniel's, said, "Parents take their kids out of school, sure. Teachers let you make up the work. But after the wildfire, Danny fell behind. We all did that year. Danny's smart, though. Or he was. We don't know what happened to him, down in New York. We all thought he was going to be a weatherman. He had a whole plan to track fires and storm cells, to help the tree growers. Guess that's not going to happen now that he's disappeared." ' "

"*That's* his plan?" Catherine asked.

"Never mind these," Lizzie said, raising her eyebrow and pushing the papers off to the side. "Tell me what happened with Christy."

Catherine's chest tightened. She stared down at the newspaper photos. The tension in Christy's face was terrible to see. "I told him," she said.

"Which part?" Lizzie said.

"That we've been helping Danny the best we can. He saw your embroidery inside Danny's hat."

"Was he mad?"

"Mad, sad, upset, all of it. I just..." Catherine began. Lizzie had shoved the papers away, but Catherine pulled them back, smoothed them out, just so she could see Christy's picture. She stared down at his face. "I just wish I hadn't hurt him."

"You can't control what Danny does, or what he wants," Lizzie said. "This is *his* family, his deal."

Catherine looked up. "You should have seen the shock in Christy's eyes when I told him. He trusted me."

"So does Danny," Lizzie said.

"How is it possible that two people who obviously feel so strongly about each other can be at such cross-purposes?"

"You mean Christy and Danny?"

Catherine nodded, blushing. Who else would she mean?

"That happens in families all the time," Lizzie said. "I have it with Lucy twelve times a day. I make oatmeal, she wants Cheerios. She wants to wear her blue socks, but I forgot to wash them. She votes for us to go to the park, and I've got my heart set on a movie and popcorn. It's one big nightmare of love."

"This isn't Cheerios and oatmeal."

"I know. It's the future of the tree farm. It's a boy breaking away from his father. It's probably a strong, silent farmer needing to say more than ten words to his kid. But I'm telling you, it *is* what happens in families. All families, in different ways."

"Why is it always so much worse at Christmastime?" Catherine asked, staring at the colored lights blinking around the mirror, at the brightly painted Santa and Christmas trees decorating the diner windows.

"Because the stakes are so much higher," Lizzie said.

"Stakes," Catherine said. "You make it sound like a game we're all betting on."

"That's exactly what we're doing," Lizzie said. "We're betting on love and happiness. And on the people who matter most. We think we have it all figured out, but when someone we care about—love with all our heart—lets us down, we lose our bets. Just look at me and Lucy's father."

Catherine nodded, squeezing her friend's hand. Lizzie had fallen in love with a man who lived in the neighborhood—Richard Thorndike, a banker down on Wall Street. Inspired by Brian, she had opened her heart to a man of commerce. Richard had renovated a loft on Fourteenth Street, and the multitalented Lizzie had been his decorator. He told her to design her dream loft, because she'd be living in it with him. Passionate about him, Lizzie had given him everything she had. When she got pregnant, she was overjoyed.

Richard Thorndike wasn't; he asked his firm for a transfer to the London office. He'd been there ever since.

"Boy, I sure lost that bet," Lizzie said. "I really should have just taken the bus to Atlantic City and put everything I had on lucky sevens. Of course I did wind up with Lucy."

"So you won big."

"Yeah, but I still felt so let down by love. As if the universe had somehow played me for a fool."

Catherine stared out the window. The snow had stopped falling, and she saw blue sky showing through swiftly moving clouds. The temperature was close to zero. Craning her neck, she tried to see Christy. He stood at the stand, stoically going about his business, trying to make up what he'd lost in the theft, she supposed.

"That's how you felt when Brian died, isn't it? And how you feel when each Christmas rolls around, and you don't see him?" Lizzie pressed.

Catherine thought of what Christy had said. "Maybe I'm not supposed to see him," she said softly. "If I saw my husband's ghost, I might want to fly away with him."

"I thought that's what you did want," Lizzie said, her mouth dropping open.

"I thought I did, too," Catherine said, staring out the window.

Danny climbed up to his secret place, looked out over the park.

Right now the sky was blue, but he knew another storm was coming. He thought about how weather was really not much more than molecules in collision; a lot like families. Blue sky didn't always mean clear sailing, and white clouds didn't always mean precipitation.

Penelope pulled on the cord he'd rigged up, and it rang the bell. Danny hurried down to let her in, and together they walked back up the narrow and circular stone stairs.

"Did you see the papers today?" she asked.

"How could I miss them?" he asked.

"My father is freaking out," she said. "I am massively grounded."

"You are?"

She nodded. "I'm supposed to be locked in the apartment, but I had to tell you. He's probably already called the cops, Danny. They'll be here any minute. You should leave if you don't want to get caught."

Danny took a deep breath, but just put his arm around her and stood his ground. "They won't get me," he said, "if I don't want them to."

"My dad's going to get you fired. He claims that you misled him and the conservancy people, applied for the job under false pretenses."

"I gave my real last name!"

"Yes, but they think your first name is Harry."

Danny grinned, knowing that Catherine would enjoy the joke.

"Not only that, but you gave some address in Chelsea for where you live. My father's on the board of the Central Park Conservancy. He'd never have recommended you for the position if he'd known you were a runaway."

"But you knew," Danny said, holding her tighter.

"I know," Penelope smiled. "I grew up sheltered, and I'm a sucker for drama. You have such a beautiful hard luck story."

Danny's smile faded. "It's not hard luck. I had an amazing upbringing. And my family is great. It's just . . . we're molecules in collision."

"Danny, people aren't clouds. I study earth science and physics, too. You're not vapor, and neither is your father."

"Just the way you said 'hard luck.' As if . . . I don't know, as if he treated me badly or something. He didn't. If anything, it's the other way around," Danny said, picturing that hurt, horrible, wrenching look on his father's face yesterday.

"Look, I didn't mean hard luck as in terrible treatment. I meant . . . you lost your mother. You come from the way-north, where I assume it's very cold. You grew up on a farm, which includes great quantities of mud and fertilizer, and where there are no yellow cabs. *That's* hard luck."

"Yeah, no yellow cabs," he said, stroking her blond hair as they both chuckled at her joke. Danny smelled her perfume. He didn't know the name, but it made his knees weak.

Sirens sounded in the distance, and Danny started. Penelope ran to look out. Danny leaned against her from behind, peering through the tower window. The park spread out around them, forests and fields bounded by the city's skyline.

Danny could never thank Penelope—or her father—enough. For most of the past year he'd had a dream job for a boy like him: clean-up kid at Belvedere Castle. Usually the position went to a student enrolled in the New York City schools, but because Danny met the qualifications and was getting his diploma through the GED, they'd made an exception.

His pay was one hundred dollars every two weeks. In return, he had to keep the information bins filled with flyers, sweep up the ones that people dropped or threw on the floor, dust the ledges, and empty the wastepaper baskets.

Belvedere Castle was designed by Frederick Law Olmsted and Calvert Vaux back in the nineteenth century, and it looked exactly like a miniature gothic stone castle, with arches and turrets, a graceful pavilion, and one tall tower topped with a flag. Danny had discovered that it was visible from just about any building bordering the park, including Penelope's apartment and Catherine's library.

The castle rose from Vista Rock, a dark cliff plunging down into Turtle Pond. The terrace attracted many park-goers, including lots of bird enthusiasts. Danny had hung around all summer and fall, enjoying especially the hawk watchers who'd gathered every morning in October to observe migrating raptors. Danny would borrow binoculars and look overhead, zeroing in on falcons, kestrels, eagles, and red-tails. He'd get a lump in his throat, wondering which birds had set off from Cape Breton.

Those hawks had seemed like harbingers of winter; if they

were overhead, it meant that Danny's father and sister couldn't be too far behind.

He had distracted himself from those thoughts by tending to his work. From here, and from his hiding place above Vista Rock, he could keep an eye on all the trees in the park. He could stare out at the Ramble, at Stone Arch, at Tupelo Meadow. He could watch dark storms rumble down the Hudson, see the golden sun rise over the East Side. He could keep track of the weather as well as any meteorologist. For Belvedere Castle was Danny's treasure trove.

Everyone who lived in New York City had often heard the words, "The temperature in Central Park is . . ." That was because the United States Weather Bureau had an outpost right there, at Belvedere Castle. Way back when they first started collecting data, in 1869, someone would take readings and telegraph them to the Smithsonian. Danny wished that was still the way! He'd give anything to be the one to read the temperature, wind speed, wind direction, visibility, air pressure, precipitation, and humidity.

Now, instead of being sent by hand, the data was taken by automated meteorological instruments. Located on the peaked roof of the castle tower and in a small fenced-in compound south of the castle, the equipment transmitted information to the U.S. Weather Bureau in Brookhaven.

Danny had ridden the Long Island Rail Road out there, back in September. He'd wanted to suggest that the bureau hire him to monitor the instruments in Central Park, supplement their readings with his own. The receptionist had smiled, giving him a form to fill out.

He'd finally met with Mr. Grant Jones in the bureau's personnel department, who'd told him that automated weather stations were now pretty much the norm, that having meteorologists on site was very rare. Danny had offered to be a fire-spotter in Central Park, like they had in some Canadian National Parks. Mr. Jones had thanked him but said that the Park Rangers and the FDNY probably had it under control with sensors and computer monitoring. Danny had ridden back to Penn Station on the train, thinking he'd better learn everything he could about computers.

Suddenly the sound of sirens got much louder, and when Danny looked out the castle window, he saw police cars zooming through the park, up the access road. They were still a way off, and he was thankful for his tower: *Belvedere* meant, after all, "beautiful view."

"Oh, God," Penelope said, leaning to see. "My father really did it."

"They won't find me," Danny said. "All they know is that I work here. They won't come up the ladder."

"They will," Penelope said miserably. "My father asked where you'd been sleeping. I didn't want to tell him, but—"

"You had to—I understand," Danny said, his stomach plummeting but not wanting her to feel bad.

"He'd figured it out anyway, Danny. Otherwise—"

"I've got to go," he said. He grabbed his knapsack, as well as Catherine's camera and the sheaf of photos he'd taken for her project. As he did, the folder spilled open, and a handful of pictures spilled out. They were of the bells Catherine had asked him about, the carved stone bells her boss had been so intrigued by. Danny had gone back to get more shots. Now, wanting to give them to Catherine, he spent a few seconds longer than he should, sweeping them up.

"Go, go," Penelope urged, peering out the window. "They'll catch you!"

"Never," Danny said, grabbing her into his arms, kissing her as if he'd never see her again.

They were in the hidden chamber just above the tower's top level. Danny had been sleeping here for months. He had the feeling that if he stayed very still right now, the police would completely miss him. Catherine's project was designed to make people "look up." To Danny and his family—people who lived out in the country—looking up was second nature. To city dwellers, Danny wasn't sure. But just in case, he shinnied up the old ladder to the very peak of the castle tower's roof.

This was how the weatherman had done it in 1869, he thought. Climbed up the ladder, out onto the roof.

The slate tiles were covered with snow and very slippery. All he had to do was stay focused, use the castle's stones as hand and footholds, just as he'd climbed cliffs at home. He'd done this exact thing before, on a full moon night last autumn, when two rangers had surprised him by following an owl into the belfry. Of course, there hadn't been any snow back then....

He suddenly heard voices, and the crackle of police radios—which spurred him on. Holding as tightly as he could to the rickety ladder, Danny imagined that he was climbing a tree. Up at home, in Nova Scotia, he would swing from one branch to another. He was at home in the trees as much as any bird. His love for the trees was in his blood, passed down from his father.

And that thought—that his father had given him his love for trees, which had led to his need to know weather—gave him an instant of pause. He pictured his father's face yesterday, so full of grief, and he realized that his dream was killing his pa.

Just then he heard a shout from the ground. He looked down—the park veered as he swayed. Had he ever climbed a tree or cliff this high before? Danny, normally fearless, felt his heart clutch. The park was lightly traveled this cold day, but he saw that a small crowd had gathered and was pointing up at him.

"Don't jump," he heard someone call.

Did they think he wanted to kill himself? *It's the opposite*, he wanted to yell back. *Love your life!*

In that moment, he lost his balance. He scrabbled for hand-holds as he sledded through the snow, grabbing at shingles, scraping his hands as he flew over the slate's sharp edges. His feet hit thin air, but his fingertips caught hold of a rusty old bracket bolted into the roof. That broke his slide.

Danny held on, his legs dangling free. It was okay, it was going to be fine . . . He would let his knapsack drop. He did—and heard it hit the ground long seconds later. His shoulders ached as he gripped the bracket, inched his body higher. If he could just get his legs up on the roof again, he could shinny up to the peak. He could pull this off—he had to. He was Harry Houdini.

But just then the rusty bracket cracked and gave way. He cried out as he tried to catch the very edge of the roof, but the ice was too slick and it happened too fast, and he heard Penelope's scream as he tumbled past the window, off the peak of Belvedere Tower.

11

Nine-one-one received twelve cell phone calls from people walking through the park, seeing a boy preparing to jump off the tower of Belvedere Castle. No other possibility occurred to them: any other explanation for a young man balanced on the snow-covered peak of the castle's tower in midday the week before Christmas would have seemed too fanciful.

Already on the scene to apprehend a reported runaway, several police officers burst into the rooftop chamber and discovered a sobbing girl clutching one single photograph of stone bells.

The officers stared down the face of dark Vista Rock. Turtle Pond was frozen with weed-choked ice. They scanned the scene, and although they didn't say it out loud, they were looking for the boy's body.

"He's dead," one officer said quietly to another, so Penelope wouldn't hear. "That's a *long* way down."

"Must be the holidays. Second suicide I've been to this week."

"The hardest time of year."

"As long as I'm not the one sent to tell his parents."

The EMTs arrived moments later, and they ran across the castle's terrace, around the stone parapet, to the place where the boy must have landed. The piles of snow were deep here—it was the dead end of a park road, where the plows dumped all excess snow, to get it off the sides of the road and keep them free for emergency vehicles. Scraped off the roadways, this snow was gray with grit, gravel, and sand.

"Hey," shouted a police officer looking down from above, up in the castle. "There's a hole in the top of that pile, right there." He pointed, and several EMTs clambered up the pile.

The officer was right—there was a huge body-shaped indentation in the very top of one deep pile. Some of the EMTs scrambled, and one radioed that they'd need shovels. They started digging out with their hands. One woman had been trained in avalanche rescue, when she worked in Utah.

No one said it out loud, but this wasn't a rescue. It was a recovery operation. It had to be. Every one of them looked up to the top of the tower and did the mental calculation. The boy had to have fallen forty feet, even allowing for the height of the pile of snow.

Still, working as if the boy's life depended on it, the emergency squad dug with all their might.

A television crew was the first news team on the scene. The girl was in shock and couldn't speak, the boy's body hadn't yet been pulled from the snow pile, and there was nothing yet in terms of an identification. The bystanders were willing to point up at the tower and tell how they'd seen a figure standing on the peak.

"He jumped," one woman said, gulping tears, "but he seemed to change his mind at the last minute. He was reaching, grabbing for anything he could hold on to. He swung there at the edge. It was awful."

The cameras showed the scene, the witnesses, and then zoomed in on the only clue to the boy's identity: the photograph of bells. Police officers said they'd had to pry the picture out of the girl's hands, that she was holding it to her heart and sobbing the words, "He thought he was a cloud."

Sylvester Rheinbeck Jr. was in his office, watching NY1 as he did most afternoons at this time. He liked the real estate report, where different city buildings were featured each day. Often they were his, making him feel proud and rich. But today his attention was grabbed by the breaking story of a boy's death in Central Park, a grave and lingering camera shot of Belvedere Castle, as well as a black-and-white photo of stone ornamentation.

The picture was of bells, and it looked familiar, very familiar. Sylvester peered at the screen. Yes, he had seen that image just a few days earlier, when his father had waxed poetic about the project he was doing with Catherine. Sylvester turned up the volume and leaned closer.

"Police have few details of who is already being called the

'Cloud Boy.' He was apparently a regular at Belvedere Castle, seeming particularly interested in the weather station here. Some are saying he was a college student, studying meteorology. Others believe—"

"Meteorology!" Sylvester murmured as the camera again showed the picture of the bells, and he began to put two and two together. He strolled down the corridor into his father's office. The old man was not there—the great room was vacant. Sylvester cast one quick look over the mahogany desk and chairs, the silver plates and cups—awards and tributes his father had received for his humanitarian works—and at the splendid views outside the window. This office really had the best vista in the tower. In fact, from here Sylvester could see the flag waving, right in the middle of Central Park, marking the top of Belvedere Castle.

Taking the private elevator, Sylvester went up to the library. His heart was pounding hard in his chest. Just as he suspected, his father was up here, sitting at a table with Catherine Tierney. They were poring over photos and contact sheets. Sylvester's mouth constricted, just a little. He shouldn't take such pleasure in what he was about to do. But he disapproved of his father's spendthrift tendencies, his improvident ways with corporate funds. And he was hurt by the way Catherine had turned him down the one time he had asked her out to dinner after her husband's death.

He walked straight in, over to the small television hidden in a wall unit. Catherine used it mainly for watching videos related to Rheinbeck Projects, but right now Sylvester Jr. tuned it to NY1. When he looked up, he saw that his father appeared very annoyed. Catherine looked beautiful but shell-shocked. As if her heart weren't quite in her work today.

"What are you doing?" his father asked.

"Remember those odd books someone left out?" Sylvester asked, staring straight at Catherine. "The ones you asked me about, Father?"

"The weather books," his father replied. "Yes, I remember taking heart when I found them. I thought perhaps you had gotten interested in something other than the prime rate."

Sylvester didn't say anything to that. He turned up the volume and let the TV reporter do the talking for him. The news had looped back to the Central Park story, with shots of the castle, police and emergency officers clustered around piles of snow, the news that a boy had fallen from the tower, and rumors that he had been hanging around the castle weather station.

"Danny!" Catherine cried, jumping to her feet.

Sylvester watched her clap her hands to her mouth. To his surprise, his father pushed himself out of his chair and put an arm around her for support. The camera panned over the picture found in the castle tower chamber—a black-and-white photo of two carved stone bells, tied together at the top with a granite ribbon.

"No, no—Danny!" she said, and Sylvester shrank from the pain in her voice. He hadn't meant to cause this kind of distress. He tried to catch his father's eye, but the old man was reaching down on the table in front of them, picking up a picture that was the mirror image of the one on TV.

Sylvester's father nodded at Catherine, his kind, steady gaze telling her to leave, do what she had to do. She flew out the door, leaving the Rheinbeck men—father and son—to face each other.

"I don't know what's going on," Sylvester said.

"You meant to show her up to me," his father said. "By pointing out the connection between those science books and the picture of the bells. I know, Sylvester. She's been letting a young man up here to use the library."

"You know, for sure?"

"Of course. Teddy, in security, reviewed the tapes. He informed me accordingly."

"And what did Catherine say?"

"I haven't mentioned it to her."

"But *why*?"

His father narrowed his eyes, took off his glasses, and removed a pumpkin-colored square of felt from his pocket to clean them with. Sylvester felt his stomach tighten. He was fifty-four years old, and he had been watching his father evade difficult questions his whole life. This is what his father did when he didn't want to answer something.

When Sylvester was seven, he had asked him to go on the father-son Adirondack camping trip, for example. Instead of saying he was too busy, his father had simply cleaned his glasses. When the company had Yankees season tickets, and Sylvester had asked if once, just once, his father could take him instead of a shareholder, his father had started polishing his lenses.

And here they were again: Sylvester asking a question, his father dismissing him with one little square of felt.

"It's against the rules," Sylvester said steadily. "We have insurance regulations. And Catherine's our employee. If she's so free about letting people up here after hours, what makes us think we can trust her not to steal—books, or funds, or corporate secrets? Some of these volumes are priceless."

"I know. They were mainly acquired by my grandfather, your great-grandfather. Remember?"

"Then you know."

"What I know, son," his father said, clearing his throat. He seemed unable to speak. Sylvester saw him reach for the felt square again, but perhaps he thought better of it. His watery blue eyes welled up.

"Father...," Sylvester began, shocked.

The old man rested one gnarled hand on Sylvester's shoulder. Late afternoon light slanted through the northwest-facing windows, throwing long shadows over the park. "What I know is that a very young man seems to have died. And that he was somehow important to Catherine Tierney. That is what I know, Sylvester."

"Yes, but—"

"All I can say, Sylvester, is that I find myself thinking. Thinking of you."

"Of me?"

"Sylvester," his father said, "if that had happened to you, I would be heartbroken. It's beyond words. Let's try to think of that boy and his family, shall we? If he is a friend of Catherine's, then he is our friend as well."

Sylvester Jr. stared at the photo of bells, and he bowed his head with shame.

Catherine walked past the choir singing "Adeste Fideles" in the Rheinbeck Tower lobby and stopped when she got to the sidewalk, crowded with Christmas shoppers. She thought of running into the park, rushing to Belvedere Castle. She wanted to be there when they found Danny. But she would only be in the way. She turned toward the subway, but she knew it would take too long. Her arm shot out. "Taxi!" she called, and a yellow cab screeched to a stop on the side of Fifth Avenue.

"Ninth Avenue and Twenty-second Street," she said, giving the address of Christy's tree stand.

The cab took off. They dodged through traffic. Catherine's heart was beating so fast, she thought she might pass out. The driver didn't give her a second glance—and why would he? She was just another passenger, in a hurry to get somewhere. He couldn't know that it was life or death.

What would she say? She hadn't seen Christy since he'd left her house. Even now she wasn't sure he'd want to speak to her. But he had to hear—she had to let him know. Maybe she was wrong, maybe the boy in the park wasn't Danny. In her heart she believed it was—and Christy would die, too, when she told him.

When the cab pulled up to his corner, she saw that he was gone. His tree stand was still set up, but the lights were out and he was nowhere to be seen. Someone must have told him. The cab driver reached for the meter to turn it off, but Catherine said, "No, not here. Please keep driving."

"Where to?" he asked.

She planned on saying her home address, on West Twentieth Street. But instead, the words that came out of her mouth shocked her.

"St. Lucy's Church," she said. "Around the corner."

"I know it," the driver said. "On Tenth Avenue."

He drove around the block, and Catherine hesitated for a moment before getting out of the cab. Her heart thudding, she gazed up at the rose sandstone church with its square bell tower where, once before, she had asked for too much.

"You okay, lady?" the driver asked.

Catherine didn't reply, but paid him his fare.

Lizzie and Lucy knelt in the back of the small church. It was dark except for blue December light coming through the stained-glass windows, and they were alone except for someone practicing Christmas music on the organ in the loft. Incense filled the air, the remnants of a late afternoon benediction. It seemed appropriate—frankincense and myrrh were two of the gifts of the Magi. On the altar was the crèche; glancing down at her daughter, Lizzie had the feeling that Lucy was praying directly to Baby Jesus, child to child. The minute Lizzie had heard the news about the boy in the park, she'd gone to get Lucy. She didn't want her hearing about Danny from anyone else.

Lucy coughed, from the incense. Her eyes were watering.

"Are you all right?" Lizzie whispered.

"Will Harry be all right, Mom?" Lucy asked now, looking up at her mother.

Oh, this was a hard one. Lizzie kept her head bowed, buying time. When Lucy was only three, she'd had to deal with the illness and death of Uncle Brian. Lizzie had worked up a whole repertoire about heaven, eternal happiness, and choirs of angels. Lucy was a very inquisitive child, and she had spent many sleepless nights grilling Lizzie on exactly where heaven was—could she show her on a map? And what was eternal happiness, and how was it better than going to the park, or for a ride on the Staten Island Ferry? And choirs of angels—well, that was fine, but what about Uncle Brian's *guardian* angel? Where was *he* when

Uncle Brian had gotten sick? What good was a guardian angel who didn't guard?

"Mommy?" Lucy whispered.

But this time Lizzie was all out of explanations. The incense thickened the air. As she knelt beside Lucy, she pressed her head to her clasped hands and felt the tears flow. Danny was so young. He had touched the dreamer in both Lizzie and Catherine. His sparkling eyes, the ferocity of his dream. She could almost see him on that roof high over the park, trying to touch the sky.

Lizzie thought of Catherine, of how, in some odd New York City miracle, Danny had brought her back to life. She had lost her faith. It was that simple. Having Brian taken from her had broken her. Catherine had shut down, stopped believing in anything, stopped believing in goodness. And then Danny had come along . . . and, this year, Christy and Bridget. Lizzie had watched her best friend open up to the Byrne family, trying, Lizzie knew, to bring them back together.

"Oh, Danny," Lizzie sobbed.

Lucy took her hand and held it. They sat like that for a long time, praying for the boy who had always been able to escape.

"Uncle Brian is taking care of him, isn't he?" Lucy asked after a long while.

Lizzie nodded. She glanced down at her amazing daughter, saw that Lucy was looking over her shoulder—toward the door.

"Mommy," Lucy whispered, tugging her sleeve.

It was Catherine.

They watched her emerge through the incense haze to stand in the back of the church, looking around as if she had never been there before. She seemed poised to run out, but instead she took a few steps forward. Something seemed to pull her toward the bank of glowing red candles, off to the right. Lizzie watched as she went over, lit a candle, and knelt at the small altar.

Lizzie's heart was in her throat. Love had never come easily to her—certainly she'd been let down by Lucy's father. But she'd always had Catherine. So much of their history could be told within the walls of this small church. They had been baptized here, made their first communions together. Catherine used to joke that Lizzie's love of hats had been formed here, that she hadn't liked any of the first communion veils and so had designed her own, using white tulle and a band of silver sequins she'd bought in the fabric district with her allowance.

That was true.

The girls had been confirmed here, and Catherine had been married here. Lizzie had been her maid of honor—they'd walked right down this aisle, and Lizzie had given her friend away to Brian, the only man Catherine swore she would ever love. And then, at Brian's funeral, Catherine had sworn to Lizzie all love had died with Brian and that she would never—ever—set foot in this place again.

And Lizzie had said a silent prayer that Catherine would find that that wasn't true. That love hadn't died, that it never could.

Staring at Catherine now, Lizzie felt her head tingle.

Somehow Lizzie knew that her prayer had been heard. Catherine knelt at the altar in front of St. Lucy, her head bowed with intensity. Lizzie closed her eyes. She saw the tree man, his son, and his daughter. They had come to New York and found Catherine just when she'd needed them most. *Don't let Danny be dead*, Lizzie prayed. *Let him have survived—and let this family come together.* Upstairs the organ was playing "Gloria in Excelsis Deo."

And Lizzie began, not so much to pray as to talk—to Brian. "Help her," Lizzie whispered. "Help her now."

She and her daughter stared, transfixed, as Catherine knelt by the small red candles. And then, holding hands, they slipped out past the crèche.

12

*W*hen *Rip came by the corner to give* Christy the news, Christy jumped straight into the squad car and sped uptown with him. Lights and sirens blaring, they zig-zagged through crazy holiday traffic, straight up Eighth Avenue.

Christy felt as if someone had reached down his throat and yanked him inside out— he felt skinned, all his nerve endings raw and wild. Rip was talking, trying to calm him down. Christy heard words, but none of them made sense. A boy had been hiding in some castle, had climbed onto the roof and jumped.

"Danny wouldn't jump," Christy said.

"He was cornered," Rip's partner said. "His hiding place found out. We closed in on him, and he must've panicked. Especially if he stole that money."

"Hey," Rip said, cautioning him.

Christy didn't care what they said. Even if Danny took the money—he had to know his father would have given it to him anyway. That was what Christy was working for, his kids. Bridget, he thought. He'd left her home, not a word. She'd be okay, she had to, but right now he had to tend to Danny.

"Here's the park," the partner said when they got to Columbus Circle. Rip drove faster. They saw other police cars, fire trucks, and ambulances. Christy's eyes swam. There weren't this many emergency vehicles in all of Cape Breton. They were all here for Danny. Surely all these people, this expensive high-performance equipment, could save the life of one young boy.

Christy's throat felt scraped raw. So many people trying to help. He saw their faces, their eyes grave and their jaws set. Trying to help. One young boy. A teenage runaway, a street kid accused of stealing his father's cashbox. Nobody important—except to Christy. Danny was the sun, the moon, and the stars to Christy. And to Bridget.

And maybe to Catherine. The thought flashed through Christy's mind, a meteor shooting so fast, he nearly missed it. She'd looked over his son this past year. The thought came, then burned away.

At one point the roadway was so jammed with emergency personnel, Rip couldn't get by. He flipped on his siren—a quick *whoop*—and tried to wave people out of the way. Christy didn't wait.

He opened the back door and jumped out. Rip yelled after him, "Christy, hang on, don't go in there!"

Christy didn't even hear. He was running as fast as he could, tearing through the crowd. The action seemed most intense off to the right, so he veered that way, off the path. Bare tree branches scraped his face. He clomped through deep snow, snagged his coat on a gorse thicket. Red and blue light strobed through the trees, painting the snow. With so many people around, there was a strange hush. No one was talking. They wouldn't—they were attending the death of a boy.

Christy's heart hammered. He wanted to get to Danny, hold him one more time. He smelled pine sap and wet bark. It felt like home here. The snow was so deep, it came over the tops of his boots. Who would ever guess this was the middle of New York City? Leave it to his son to find nature.

Leave it to his son to find the best things anywhere. Danny had found this park: wide open spaces, a city forest, owls calling from the treetops. Danny had found the things he'd needed to survive this year without his family. Catherine. She'd kept him going till now.

Christy's chest tightened. He smashed his way through the snow, saw the castle looming up ahead, circled around to where he saw the emergency workers congregated. The castle was built high on a massive cliff, right by a pond, so divers stood on the bank, awaiting orders to take over for the ones already under water. The police had formed a perimeter—he saw yellow tape and a line of officers. Christy didn't stop, didn't even pause, just shouldered his way through.

A cop laid hands on him. Christy shook him off like a mosquito in the woods. He saw the pile of snow up ahead. Workers were digging with shovels and picks. Christy clambered down the rock, then up the snow-hill, brushing people aside. A pair of police ran up after him, grabbed him from behind, and Christy just wrenched himself free.

Rip shouted out—Christy registered the familiar voice, but he was beyond hearing. He made it to the top of the snow heap, looked down. There had been a hole, but the sides had caved in on itself, smothering whoever was inside. Traces of blood smeared the snow.

Danny's blood.

Other people were shouting to get Christy away, but the louder they yelled, the quieter he felt.

When Christy Byrne started digging for his son's body, he was as silent as the forest itself. As silent as the hillside where he grew trees and raised his children, overlooking the cold northern bays, dazzled by the aurora borealis. As silent as all that.

Christy dug.

The church was cold.

St. Lucy's was not a rich parish, and the pastor tried to save money by not turning the heat up except during mass. The air was thick with incense and made Catherine cough. She knelt in front of the candles. Her face and clasped hands felt warm from the flames. Even so, she was shivering.

This felt so strange. To be drawn back to a place that had once meant so much to her. The very air had once felt charged with hope, with the belief that miracles happened every day. Catherine had led a blessed life. She had had parents who loved her, a best friend who was just like a sister, and one true love. Brian.

During their marriage he had gotten her to work at St. Lucy's, giving up big segments of her time for the hungry and poor. She would kneel in this church with Brian, and she would know that their love was so huge it could change lives, help people. The rose window would crackle with colored light; the smell of incense would make her swoon. Catherine would feel wildly alive with faith and love.

Now the church was just a building.

A cold building at that. Catherine glanced around: four walls, brightly colored stained glass windows, a white dove high above the marble altar. These candles, and this statue of Saint Lucy. The smell of incense mixed with the candle smoke. She peered through the haze. Why had Catherine wasted the time coming here? Someone else she loved had died. Danny.

"Why?" she whispered.

Nothing but silence. What had she expected?

"I tried to help him. I tried to do what you wanted. You always said we had so much. . . . That we had to give back."

The organist had stopped playing, slipped out behind Catherine. She felt the chill as the heavy church door opened and closed. The incense was so strong. Catherine had never smelled it like this before. *Gifts of the Magi*, she thought. As children, she and Lizzie had loved the words of Matthew 2:11: *"And entering the house, they found the child with Mary his mother, and falling down they adored him: and opening their treasures, they offered him gifts: gold, frankincense, and myrrh."*

Frankincense for the baby, for the family.

The candle flames flickered. She blinked, staring at the sparkling red votives. She thought of gifts . . . something to give, for Danny, for Christmas, for help. A gift for the family . . . Digging in her pocketbook, she pulled out her wallet. There it was, her picture of Brian. Propping the photo up against the statue of

Saint Lucy, she stared at it. She blinked away smoke, and her eyes teared up.

"He was so alone," she whispered. "Only seventeen, alone in New York City. He never asked for help; we had to nearly force him to take it. He turned seventeen here, not even two months ago. His family loved him, missed him so much. They never got to say good-bye. At least I got to say good-bye to *you*."

The breeze came again, stronger this time. Catherine's hair blew into her face, brushed across her tears. "You promised you'd never leave. I've looked for you every Christmas. I've waited for you in our house, up in the attic... Brian..."

You were waiting in the wrong place.

Catherine wheeled around. She heard the words, as clearly as if Brian himself had spoken them. Surely, it was his voice. She sprang up, followed it toward the altar. Here the air was so thick, she could hardly see through the fragrant smoke of the Magi's gift, the incense. The psalm came back to her, *"I have cried to Thee, O Lord, hear me: hearken to my voice, when I cry to Thee. Let my prayer be directed as incense in Thy sight; the lifting up of my hands, as evening sacrifice."*

"Please, please," she prayed.

The incense burned in a bronze thurible, suspended by chains beside the main altar, above the crèche. She held her breath, blinking away the smoke. Her husband was standing there, shimmering behind the haze, reaching out his hand. Shocked, she couldn't move. He smiled at her with endless, eternal love—such depth of love in his warm green eyes that she felt ashamed for ever doubting.

"Brian," she whispered. "Oh, my God, it's you!" she said, reaching toward him, wanting to touch his cheek. But she stopped just short. Was he there? Was this a dream? She blinked, trying to see through the veil of smoke.

"Help me tonight," she begged. "Danny's in such danger. Please, for Christmas, you always said you'd be here. Come tonight, Brian. We need you!"

She saw a dazzling brightness standing beside the crèche. His eyes, his smile... the smoky haze made her doubt her own vision. For although Brian was right there, he seemed almost to shimmer, as if he were made of fog.

"It's you, it has to be," she whispered. "Because I need your help. Tonight, of all nights, Brian. You taught me to see what others need. There's a boy and his family, suffering so... Brian, what can I do?"

I can't tell you, she heard. *I can only show you.*

His image wavered, disappeared, as it had so many times during these last years, when she had seen him in the mist, in the snow, in her dreams.

"Oh, please," she cried. "Don't go!"

Someone touched her hand then, and she felt a shock pass through her body—it rattled her bones, and although it was extreme, it didn't hurt. When it stopped, she looked down at herself. She was like a shadow, like Brian. She was vapor. And then, just as suddenly, she was solid again. The incense was playing a trick on her eyes. But suddenly she knew for sure, without any doubt, that Brian was with her.

She felt shaken, but she wasn't scared. Waves of love passed through her. A cold blast of air blew through the church, clearing the incense. When the smoke dissipated, she followed the wind out the back door, into the night. The wind blew across Tenth Avenue, and she ran after it.

"There's not time," she called. "Danny needs us *now*."

But the wind ignored her, blowing harder, faster, making the snow swirl on the sidewalk just ahead of her footsteps.

On Twentieth Street, Catherine felt a swoop of vertigo, and she clutched for something to hold on to—a ginkgo tree growing out of the sidewalk, the iron rail of her neighbor's yard. Her heart pounded, and she knew she was following Brian. His ghost was here tonight, leading her where she had to go.

As always at Christmas, her street seemed shrouded in mist. Catherine peered through it, seeing spirits in the air. An arm slid around her waist, leading her to her own front steps. She gasped, and when she dared breathe and glance over, she saw a flash of wings. Spectacular white feathered wings, just like an archangel's.

Hands shaking, she unlocked her door. The wind swirled through her front door, scattering mail and the morning paper. It blew upstairs, and she followed it, all four stories, into the attic. Her mind raced with everything he had missed since they'd parted, all the things she wanted to tell him.

"Three years I waited for you here," she said, flying into the room. It was so cold. She had turned the heat down, and her breath came out in clouds. He wasn't here. She'd been imagining . . . but as she wheeled around, she caught sight of him in the cheval glass in the corner. His shape glowed. Catherine gasped, walking closer.

She saw her husband's reflection, shimmering in the glass.

"Brian," she said. "Please . . . talk to me. You couldn't come to me here . . . you said this was the wrong place?"

I brought you back here tonight because this is where we loved each other, she heard.

"We did," she breathed, trying to touch his face in the glass. "You knew how much I wanted to live here; you bought this house for me. We filled it with our love for each other." She gestured at all the framed pictures—of their wedding, their honeymoon in Paris, Lucy's christening, museum galas, wearing aprons at the soup kitchen, decorating their last Christmas tree together.

And for the last three years, until this season, you've filled it with your sadness.

Catherine's heart beat faster, and she tried to touch his face in the glass. The reflection shimmered under her fingers. She welled up, trying to get his face to come into clearer focus. "I've missed you so much," she said.

Catherine felt the tears running down her cheeks. The mist began to thicken again as she gazed into the glass. She felt amazing peace and steadiness, and began to feel calm. She had wanted help for Danny, but suddenly she knew that first she and Brian had to say good-bye.

She reached toward the mottled glass—and stars sparked when her fingers touched. She closed her eyes, pressing her cheek against the cold surface.

"We've had three years to get ready for this," she whispered. "That's what this is, isn't it? Tonight is our time to say good-bye. Really good-bye, so that I can move on in life. And you can . . . move on in death. I love you, Brian."

I'll always love you, Catherine. Love never dies. The voice was real. Catherine felt the warmth of his skin, the strength of his arms. Her body swayed. Had time stood still, or had it evaporated? Had any of the last hour really happened? She cried, holding on tight. If she didn't let him go—if this time she held on forever . . . She felt their hearts beating together, and something inside her chest released. She felt as if doves had flown out of her body, filling the room with their wing beats.

"Brian," she cried out. "Help me find a way to help Danny . . ."

You know what to do, she heard.

She closed her eyes. In her mind, she saw it all. He held out his hand, and she took it. He spread his wings, and she wasn't afraid. She had a vision: they flew out the small attic window, over the darkened seminary heath, the former farmland where Clement Clarke Moore had penned his Christmas poem. They circled over Christy's abandoned tree stand, through Chelsea, over the avenues and buildings of midtown, through the red-and-green glow of the Empire State Building, all the way to Central Park.

When she opened her eyes, she was still in the attic room.

"Brian?" she asked.

But he was gone. Catherine ran down the four flights, grabbed her coat, and dashed out the door. She ran through the snow, slipping once, falling to her knees. Her eyes darted back and forth—it was a night for angels and ghosts.

Hailing a cab, she had him drive her uptown to the park. Her heart lurched, drawing close to the castle tower. She saw all the emergency vehicles, the truck from the morgue. Tavern on the Green glowed with holiday lights, and horse-drawn carriages jingled with sleigh bells.

"Brian," she said out loud, in the backseat of the cab.

"Never let Christmas be a sad time again," the driver said, looking at her in the rearview mirror.

"Who are you?" she gasped, seeing Brian's eyes reflected there.

The driver laughed quietly as they drove unimpeded through the police and emergency vehicles, straight into the woods bordering Turtle Pond. "Don't you know a miracle when you see one?"

"You mean?" she asked, touching the driver's shoulder.

"Go find them," Brian said. He touched her hand, and she felt her skin and bones rattle, her blood rush into her head. "Don't forget..."

"Don't forget what?"

"To look up," he said. And with one burst of flight, of dazzling white feathers, he was gone.

Catherine stared up at the sky. All she could see were clouds moving in fast, covering the stars. The night was dark and freezing cold. Icicles hung from the tree branches, and snow flurries began to fall. She turned toward the castle.

The pile of snow that Catherine had seen on television had dwindled to almost nothing, dug all the way down to the ground from the very top of Vista Rock. What had once been twenty feet deep was now a quarter that. She ran toward it. Workers leaned on their shovels, sweaty with exertion. They stared at the snow pile, watching one single man continue to dig.

"Christy!" she yelled.

"Leave him," one cop said to her. "It's the boy's father—he's out of his mind."

Catherine wrenched free. She tore to the snow pile, began scrambling up. Christy was in there, digging with his hands. His blue eyes were both wild and weary. At the sight of Catherine, they filled, and tears streaked down his grimy face.

"Stop, Christy," she said.

"I can't," he said, his voice breaking. "Not till I find Danny."

"You won't find him there," she said, reaching out her arm. Her hand was right there—all he had to do was take it. He stared at her hand, her fingers. His expression was defeated, as if he'd forgotten the meaning of hope. His gaze was blunted, beaten down. But when he looked into Catherine's, he must have seen something that gave him a start.

Her own eyes were sparkling—she could feel it.

She left her hand there for the longest time, until Christy was ready to take it. He did, finally. She used all her strength to pull him out of the hole. It was rimmed with bits of gravel, traces of blood—and thousands of small white feathers. As Christy stood there, shaking and shivering, she took him in her arms.

"We have to go," she said.

"But where? How can I leave without Danny?" he asked.

"You could *never* leave without Danny," she said. "Come on. Let's go find your son."

$\mathcal{B}$ridget sat on the sofa, holding $\mathcal{M}$urphy on her lap, doing her best to block out the sound of the TV in the other room. Mrs. Quinn had the volume on very low, probably because she didn't want to upset her. Well, she *was* upset. Bridget just concentrated on holding Murphy and listening to the snow that had started to fall and trying not to go crazy over what had happened to her brother.

Lizzie and Lucy had been here for a while, and Bridget had liked that, because they didn't talk about Danny or what was happening. Lizzie had brought yarn over, to show Bridget and Lucy how to knit. They just kept her company, quietly knitting, until it was time to get Lucy home for bed. Bridget liked the soothing, repetitive motion of knit-one, purl-one, knit-one, purl-one, but after they left, her thoughts were too wild for her to concentrate on knitting.

At about nine-thirty the door swung open, and Mrs. Quinn stepped in, carrying a tray from the kitchen. It was laden with hot milk in a small blue-flowered pot, a matching cup, some oatmeal cookies, and a cut-up apple.

"I see you have Murphy keeping you company," Mrs. Quinn said. "And your knitting is really coming along."

Bridget glanced down at her needles and three inches of a skinny green scarf. She felt too upset to say a word, and as if Murphy knew, she craned up and licked her chin. The gesture made Bridget tremble. Her brother used to laugh when the terrier did that to him.

"I thought maybe you could use a snack."

"I'm not hungry," Bridget managed.

Mrs. Quinn was tall and thin. She had expressive blue eyes, white hair pulled back into a bun, and a quick smile that often turned into a laugh. Right now even Mrs. Quinn couldn't smile. She stood there in her black dress, with the olive green cardigan that used to be her husband's pulled over her shoulders, staring down at Bridget with a deep grandmotherly gaze.

"You need to keep your strength up," Mrs. Quinn said. "Have just a bite of apple."

"Not till I know," Bridget said. Again Murphy licked her chin. Mrs. Quinn stared at her for a few long seconds. They ticked by, and Bridget wished she would go back into her quarters. Not because Bridget didn't like her, but because the door to her room was open and Bridget could hear the TV talking about Danny.

Finally, Mrs. Quinn patted her gently on the head and returned to her rooms, pulling the door shut behind her. Bridget tried to pick up her knitting again. The needles felt solid in her fingers. She liked the idea of making something, having it grow with every stitch. In a way, it was like farming trees. Start with a seed, or one stitch, and watch it get bigger.

Bridget stared at her knitting. If Danny was still alive, the scarf would be for him. She'd give him everything she had. If only her father hadn't fought him so hard last year. If only he could have talked to Danny, reasoned things out with him. Maybe none of this would be happening!

She knew that December was flying by. Next week was Christmas, and she and her father would be returning to Nova Scotia, to their farm way at the very north of Cape Breton. So far from New York City . . . so far from Danny.

The snow began falling harder. It obliterated the streetlights and looked like an orange blur, almost like a blizzard, just as it had the other night, when her father had gone chasing after Danny. He thought Bridget hadn't seen, but she had heard him bellow her brother's name: *Danny!*

And peering out the window, she had seen her brother jump on the M11 bus and pull away, with their father picking up the dropped hat, then running down the middle of the street behind the bus. She shook her head now, starting to knit. Until they told her Danny was dead, she wouldn't believe it. Even then, she might not believe it. All she could do was sit here and knit her brother a scarf.

Her needles clicked, and so did the snow against the windows. The clicking seemed to get louder, ice crystals in the flakes. Or . . .

Something really loud clunked against the alley window. Murphy jumped up on the armchair to see out, barking. Bridget flew off the sofa, scattering her needles and yarn.

"What was that?" Mrs. Quinn called.

"Danny," Bridget whispered, her heart exploding as she stared out the window into the dark alley below.

Danny stood between the buildings, looking up at the bright windows above. He saw his sister's face, the most welcome sight in the world. She motioned that she'd be right down. He felt weak and pale, as if he wasn't quite right in his body. He was hovering inches above the ground. He felt like a sleepwalker. When he blinked, he saw stars.

He leaned against one of the buildings, feeling the cold of the brick penetrate his thick down jacket. He had taped up last year's tear, from where his father had grabbed his sleeve. And now he'd have to do the same again. Somewhere in the tumble he'd taken, he'd snagged his side, and half the feathers had gone flying. The snow pile had broken his fall, but he'd cut his wrist—and his head, too.

A door slammed, and he heard small footsteps running toward him. It was Bridget. She came down the alley with the compact force of a pilot whale, jumping into his arms and pinning him against the building.

"Danny, oh Danny," she cried.

"Whoa, Bridey," he said.

"I thought, we all thought . . . ," she sobbed.

Danny held her, trying to steady himself. He had to think. Those cops at the castle had really wanted to catch him. He knew that he was in trouble for some really serious things, nearly all of which he'd done. He had wrongfully inhabited Belvedere Castle, breaking lots of Central Park rules and city laws. Penelope's father hated him now, for abusing their trust. He just really hoped Penelope wouldn't get blamed for what he'd done. And then there was the money they were saying he stole.

"Where's Pa?" he asked his sister.

"He's at the park!"

Danny shook his head, trying to clear it. What was she talking about?

"What's he doing there?" he asked.

Bridey pushed back, giving him a look of incredulity. "He's looking for you. He's waiting for them to find your body."

"My *what*?" Danny asked. Shocked, he had to lean against the wall again.

"They think you're dead," she said. "People saw you jump from the top of that castle."

"I didn't jump."

"I know that. Pa does, too. We thought you fell."

"I did," Danny said. "And I landed right in this big, soft snow-bank. I couldn't even believe it myself. I felt the impact and thought that was it. But I climbed out..."

"Your head..." Bridey said, reaching up. Her fingers touched the cut, and Danny flinched.

"I'm really in trouble," he said, talking fast and feeling dizzy with his sister's news. "They think I stole Pa's tree money. Did you see the newspapers? You must have."

"I'm so sorry about that," she whispered.

"Why? You know I didn't do it, don't you, Bridey? And Pa knows, right? Tell me he knows."

"I think he thinks . . ." Bridget said, trailing off.

"Tell me he knows me better than that," Danny said. "Oh Bridey, he doesn't think I'd steal from him, does he? I'd never do that!"

"He thinks your life on the street was so terrible, that you needed the money to take care of yourself," she said, her voice shaking. "He'd give it to you anyway, we both would. We love you so much, Danny."

His head had really started to bleed again, trickling into his eyes. He pressed the sleeve of his jacket to the wound. It felt warm and sticky. Danny knew that cuts to the head always bled the most.

He remembered seeing his pa get hit with a falling branch once, during a surprise storm. They'd had no advance warning— it had been sunny and calm one minute, then dark and windy the next. His father had been pruning trees when the windstorm struck with brutal force. If only they'd had some preparation, maybe his father wouldn't have been up the tree. Danny was six years old, and he'd cried really hard because of all the blood coming from his father's head. He had thought his father was going to die.

And that memory was like a burst of cold water.

"Pa thinks I'm dead?" he asked.

"We all did."

"I've got to go find him," Danny said, remembering that terror he'd felt so many years ago, thinking he was going to see his father die of that head wound. "Let him know it's not true."

Grabbing for his sister's hand, he realized she was holding a pillowcase full of things. "What's this?" he asked.

"I brought you cookies and an apple and some of Pa's dry

socks, things you need," she said, her eyes glittering in the street-light.

Danny put his arm around her. He couldn't think or take it all in. His head was spinning, and his wrist and head hurt. His whole left side felt bruised. His sister was crying, and Danny knew that he had done it to her.

"Let's go," Danny said.

"Where?"

"To find Pa," he said.

A shadow fell across the streetlight, and they heard footsteps in the alley. Danny shaded his head to see who was coming. He flinched, thinking maybe it was the police. But it wasn't. No one said a word. Danny just saw his face, shadowed by the snowy light, and he felt his father's huge embrace.

His father just stood there and rocked him in the snow.

When Christy could register the reality of it, the fact that his son was alive, he took his arms away and stood back to make sure it was really true. There Danny stood. It was really him. Christy glanced over at Catherine to make sure she saw the same thing. She did—she was beaming. How had she known? How could Danny have survived that fall?

"You're hurt," he said, turning back to his son, touching his head.

"He's bleeding a lot, Pa," Bridget said.

"I cut my wrist on the roof," he said. "And I think I scraped my head on the snowbank. And tore my jacket."

"I saw the feathers," Christy said. "And the blood."

"And you thought I was dead in there?"

"You're lucky, Danny—it was so deep."

Overwhelmed with the miracle of it, Christy grabbed him close again. He hadn't held his son in a year—the last time had been that terrible fight, when Danny had been trying to get away. And now here they were, standing together, practically in the same spot. Christy couldn't believe it—his son had come back. Just yesterday he had run away from him, right across the street at the bus stop. Christy flashed on the cashbox, but he couldn't bring himself to think of it now. He just looked across the top of Danny's head and saw Catherine with her eyes closed, as if in gratitude for this moment.

"We have to get you to a doctor," Christy said.

"I'm fine."

"Your father's right," Catherine said. She stepped forward and touched Danny's cheek with such affection, Christy could see that they knew each other, and that Danny trusted her very much. Her eyes were luminous, full of mystery and reflection, reminding him of northern bays. He stood beside her, and seeing her caress his son's face made his heart melt. "You're hurt, Danny," she said.

"It's nothing, C. I saw Pa get hurt much worse, a hundred times. He always just shakes it off. That time with the tree branch, Pa. After that cold front rolled in so fast? Remember?"

"Let's go to a hospital," Christy said.

"Pa, the weather changed so fast—you had no warning. You got hurt. I thought you might die. Remember?"

"The weather—what does that matter? It just *is*. Come on, Danny, now . . ." Christy said, shocked by Danny's expression—he was hanging on to Christy's sleeve, insistent, refusing to move. Suddenly Christy's stomach dropped. Was this what it was all about? His son's desire to know about weather? Because this was a magical night, Christy's mind was crackling with awareness. He wanted to know what had pulled his family apart, and what was drawing them back together. He wanted to know Danny.

"You live by the sword every day," Danny said, his voice cracking. "That's what it's like out on the hill, with the wind and the ice, and the heat and the fires. Someone has to help you, Pa. And I don't mean just by planting and cutting."

"We have to help each *other*," Bridget suddenly screamed.

"Bridey," Danny said.

"We can't be apart anymore!" Flinging herself toward her brother, she let go of the pillowcase that—until now—Christy hadn't even noticed. It fell to the ground, and all the contents spilled out.

A napkin filled with Mrs. Quinn's cookies, a cut-up apple turning brown around the edges, a few pairs of Christy's rolled-up socks, and the cashbox.

"It was for Danny," Bridget sobbed. "I couldn't bear to think of him living alone here—all by himself in this city. Going to the soup kitchen, sleeping wherever he could. I wanted him to be safe and fed."

"Sweetheart," Christy said, reaching for her in shock.

But she pulled back. She was only twelve, but the strength in her eyes shot a bolt right through him. "I'm sorry, Pa," she said. "I shouldn't have taken it. But I love my brother, and I'd do anything for him. He can't come back to the farm with us, because he has to become a weatherman. He has to stay here."

"We'll figure that out—" Christy began.

"Danny," Catherine said, stepping toward him, putting her arms around him.

Christy grabbed Danny, seeing that he was losing his balance. He picked his grown son right up into his arms, the way he used to when Danny was a baby. His head was reeling, the whole world was rocked, but for now all he knew was that he had to get Danny to a hospital.

14

*W*e stitched his head, and he has a concussion," the doctor said, standing in the emergency room at St. Vincent's Hospital. "And we're concerned about the possibility of internal injuries. He's a lucky young man to have survived that fall."

"What kind of internal injuries?" Christy asked.

"We're running tests. We'd like to keep him for observation."

Christy stood there stubbornly. Now that he had his boy back, he didn't want to leave him for a minute. The police had asked their questions, reporters were lingering outside. New York City welfare agencies had sent people to investigate. They were talking about taking the kids away, filing criminal charges against Danny, maybe arresting Christy for neglect.

Christy wanted to go into the ER cubicle where Danny lay, bundle him up, and take him back home—tonight. He had to get him away from New York, had to leave this city that had caused him and his family so much trouble. He felt like a wounded buck: shot, backed into a corner, ready to fight to the death to get free.

"You have to let him stay," Catherine said.

"They're talking about arresting him."

"They won't arrest him, Christy."

"How do you know? How can you say? They're after us. Can't you see the way those cops looked at me? As if I'm the worst scum in the world? One kid ran away from me, the other has to steal to get what she needs for her brother—" He broke off. Why couldn't Rip have been the one questioning him? Because it wasn't his precinct, his jurisdiction. Everything in New York came with rules, regulations, boundaries foreign to Christy. His mouth was bone dry, his skin crawling. He was on high alert, feeling under attack.

"I know," Catherine said calmly. "All he did was sleep there, at the castle. He didn't steal anything, hurt anybody."

"They're saying—" Christy choked up. He knew the story behind the story was that last year he had hit Danny, that charges had been filed and dropped. He was so afraid that the law would paint his son with the same brush—two no-good Canadians causing trouble on the streets.

"Christy," Catherine said, "just concentrate on him getting care. Let him stay in the hospital."

"Then I'm staying with him."

"You should go home and get some rest," said the doctor, who had been standing off to the side. "He has a long night of tests ahead of him."

"I'm staying," Christy growled.

"As you like," the doctor said. "We don't have room on the floor yet, so we're keeping him in the ER. You'll have to wait here, in the waiting room."

It was two in the morning. Catherine stood beside him; she hadn't left him for a minute, except to call Lizzie around midnight and ask her to come and pick up Bridget. Christy had registered the ease with which Catherine could ask her friend for help, and the willingness of Lizzie and Lucy to get up in the middle of the night. He thought of his daughter screaming out "we have to help each *other,*" and the memory rifted his heart—a tree being pulled out by its roots. Bridget—how had he missed what she was going through? He'd never seen her like that, mad with panic, wanting to pull her family together.

Christy looked at Catherine. Her clear gray eyes were fixed on him. As she stared back at him, he blinked and looked away. He felt so confused by the night's events, by both of his children's behavior, and by his own feelings about it all. Worrying about the city coming in, taking the kids from him, drove him to the brink of madness.

As if Catherine could read his terror, she touched his arm. He felt a shiver quake through his body. He wanted to hold her right here in the bright, seething waiting room of St. Vincent's ER. Her body against his, as it had been just nights ago, one with each other. But tonight was a nightmare he had to get through alone.

"Thank you for everything, but go on home now," he said. His voice shook. Could she see the tremor in his hands? As strong and stern as he sounded, inside he was the opposite. He was falling apart, right at her feet.

"That's okay," she said, seeing right through him. "I'll stay with you."

He tried to catch his breath.

"But why?" he said. "I don't understand. What do we mean to you? We're just tree people from Canada. My kids—look at my kids. The questions the cops ask tell you what they think of us. Danny ran away from me, Bridget stole the money I earned. What a terrible person I must be."

But Catherine was looking at him as if she thought he was anything but terrible. Her lucent eyes were still and grave, clear as calm water.

"Weren't you listening?" she asked. "Danny wants to become a meteorologist for *you*. Because he knows how dangerous the weather can be on the farm. And Bridget took that money to give to Danny. You all want to help each other. You just have to figure out how."

"What if they take them away from me?" he whispered. "What if that's what happens when morning comes?"

"They won't. We won't let them."

We.

Christy stared at her. He remembered that night in the front hall of her brick house, holding her. In that one moment, everything had slipped away—the facts and realities and the differences between them. All he'd felt was the tilt of the earth on its axis, the two of them hurtling through space together, the solidity of her body against his, the crash of their hearts together. That's all he had felt.

"Just tell me," he said now. "Why do you care about us? Why are you here right now?"

"Why did you invite me sledding with you? Why did you trust me to take Bridget to see the tree lighting?" she countered, her gray eyes glinting. "Who can explain connection? Why should we even try?"

Christy gazed at her, hard. Something had changed since that night in her house. She had seemed too vulnerable then—pulled away from herself and the Christmas season, haunted by the specter of her husband. Right now the bruised sadness in her eyes was gone. She looked radiant, as fierce as a warrior.

"What happened tonight?" he asked.

"You and Danny found each other again," she said.

"No, something else. I can see it in your eyes."

She glanced from side to side. There were so many people close by. He saw her holding herself back. His stomach flipped, as if he'd fallen out of a tree.

"If it has to do with Danny, you have to tell me."

"I will," she said. "But not here."

Christy was in a free fall. Tonight should be the happiest night of his life. Danny had survived catastrophe. His family was re-united, for the moment anyway. And Catherine was here beside him. Her nearness and warmth sent hot chills through him, made him want to hold her again.

But his pulse was racing, every heartbeat filling his body with fear. Christy was a simple farmer. He was motivated by old hunger, a childhood of "not enough," and his drive was toward feeding his family, taking care of business, growing Christmas trees to put bread on the table. Catherine had such *layers*. She was a sophisticated Manhattanite with ways as mysterious to Christy as those of Byzantium. The fact that she could hold back information about things she knew about his son scared him.

"You'd better go now," he said.

"Christy," she said.

"You've done enough for us," he said. "We're grateful. Don't think we're not. But I can handle this now. I have to. They're my children, and I have to fight for them."

"I'll stand alongside you."

"But it's not," he said in a rough, husky voice, "your fight."

She opened her mouth, as if to argue. But then she caught sight of something—the total panic and terror in his eyes, maybe. He saw her make peace with herself. He had the feeling maybe she knew it would upset him more if she stayed. Nodding reluctantly, she leaned forward, kissed him on the cheek. His whole side burned at the brush of her lips, her hand. He watched her go, more confused than he'd ever felt in his life.

Christy swallowed. He found one empty chair in the crowded room. People with cuts, bad coughs, wasted eyes, sick babies, bad limps, bandaged hands surrounded him. Some of them were homeless. Christy could tell by their holey shoes and filthy coats. How would they all pay for their medical care? How would Danny have paid, if he were alone?

Alone. The word had a terrifying ring to it. *Alone, alone.* It sounded like a funeral bell, like the bell buoy in Wolf Strait, marking treacherous shoal water. Christy gazed around the room, looking at all the people without anyone by their sides. An artificial tree stood in a corner, flashing with colored lights. Cardboard cutouts of snowmen and candy canes hung on the walls.

Christy stared at the tree. Everything about it bothered him. It was fake. It was crooked, from being in storage the year before. The branches were askew. There wasn't any pine scent. The needles were too long and green. It was trying too hard to bring cheer, but it couldn't deliver. It was a phony. Christy felt that way himself. He was the salesman with a golden tongue, trying to sell Christmas to all the rich New Yorkers.

While his own family was hanging in tatters.

Christy looked at the chair beside him. Catherine wasn't in it. Christy didn't know his own children. *Alone, alone,* he thought as the lights on the fake tree blinked and blinked.

Catherine caught a cab and went home. When she got there, she ran straight up to the attic room. It was empty. A cold draft blew through the small window. She looked around, but without any worry or anxiety. She and Brian had said good-bye. She knew that her husband had gone for good.

Brian had his journey to make, and Catherine had hers.

It had started tonight, on the perimeter of all those emergency workers at Belvedere Castle. She had burst through, needing to get to Christy. When she'd seen that snow pile, with its scattering of white feathers, she had known: others might think the down came from Danny's jacket, but Catherine knew they'd come from Brian.

Brian's wings.

Somehow Brian and his love—their love—had survived after all. And she knew now that it wouldn't die. Their love would live on. They had flown through the night; he had brought her here, to this room on the very top floor of their townhouse, because this was where they had known such love. That was the only explanation for why she had chased the wind up here, followed the flash of white wings.

Catherine stood in the room, slowly turning. She suddenly knew that a person couldn't be ready one minute before the time was right. She looked at every picture on the wall, taking each down, holding each in her hands. She and Brian at the beach, at Yankee Stadium, after their wedding . . . on the steps at St. Lucy's.

Staring at the picture, something sparked. What was it? Everything in the photo was so familiar—Brian's smile, his playful eyes, her own expression of joy, the church itself. She scanned the building: its rose sandstone facade, the stained glass windows, the square bell tower. It reminded her of some of the medieval churches they'd seen on their honeymoon.

The picture seemed to give off electricity. Catherine looked at the church, thinking of how she had gone inside tonight, for the first time in three years. She could almost see the candles flickering, the red votives, the thick incense. She had knelt at the small back altar, under the loving gaze of Saint Lucy herself. She had followed her husband's voice into the fragrant drift of incense, up to the thurible suspended by the crèche, where the cloud was thickest.

What did it all mean? The veil seemed so thin, between people and angels, between the living and the dead. Why, after so many seasons of waiting for Brian right here, in this room, had she seen him at church instead? Was it something about St. Lucy's? Or was it just that Catherine needed to leave her home, this wonderful place that had become her cave? She had imprisoned herself in grief here.

Examining the picture, she felt her heart pounding. It wasn't every night that a miracle occurred—Brian's visit, Danny's saving.

She closed her eyes and thought of Danny in the hospital, Bridget in the twin bed beside Lucy's, Christy in the ER waiting room. She wondered whether any of them were getting sleep tonight. She knew that they were all worried about what tomorrow would bring.

"Let the right thing happen," she prayed.

She kissed Brian's face—her bridegroom. Then she replaced the picture on the wall and took a deep breath. She wasn't sad; she had already said her good-byes. Walking over to the window, she peered down at the street. What would people think when they looked up in the future? Would they imagine that a happy family lived here? That this small room was the nursery?

Would they be right?

Catherine couldn't know. A leap of faith wasn't a reach from point A to point B: it was a leap into the dark, and the unknown. It was lighting a candle and summoning your husband's ghost. It was being blown by an unexpected wind from a tall tree, sparking the desire in your son to become a weatherman. It was climbing the castle tower, falling into the arms of an angel. It was knowing that your family hung in the balance, waiting for others to decide its fate.

And now, for Catherine, it was waiting for what would happen next; that was the biggest leap of faith of all.

She took one last look around the room. She knew that this was the last time she would come up here. Breathing in, she waited to feel sad. But she didn't, not at all. Instead she felt filled with exultant joy. There was hope, and Catherine felt it. She was ready. Her time had come.

Locking the door behind her, she walked down the stairs to wait.

Once again the newspapers carried the story of Christy Byrne and his family. All through New York City people read the tale of a boy who had survived a plunge from the tower of Belvedere Castle. The threads all came together: Daniel Byrne was the son of the tree salesman, Christopher Byrne, of Pleasant Bay, Nova Scotia, whose money had been stolen just the day before.

All the way from the northernmost reaches of Cape Breton, the Byrne family had traveled, year after year, to New York, to ply their trade and sell their trees. Although Daniel's escape from death was nothing less than miraculous, the Byrne saga was in many ways tragic. Daniel was a runaway, one of the city's desperate homeless. His sister Bridget had confessed to stealing her father's cashbox and the thousands of dollars it contained.

Family services were investigating. Foster care was being considered. Criminal charges were pending—against Daniel Byrne, for a variety of offenses ranging from trespassing to theft; against his father, for child neglect; possibly against Bridget, for theft.

Sitting in his office, Sylvester Rheinbeck Sr. adjusted his gold spectacles and read every word of every article about Daniel Byrne. He paid particular attention to the paragraph in the *New York Times* article that stated, "Lost in this story of holiday joy and sorrow is the mysterious picture of stone bells. Police are investigating the possibility that Daniel Byrne had at one time been employed by the Rheinbeck Group, as part of their philanthropic 'Look-Up Project.' A company spokesman denies any such connection."

Sylvester Sr. shook his head. Only the venerable, stodgy *Times* would say the story of the bells had been "lost." Quite the contrary: according to company gossip, which Sylvester trusted far more than the *New York Times*, the bells were becoming a city-wide obsession. "The Miracle of the Bells," some people were calling it. Where *were* the stone bells? Why had the boy had a picture of them? The bells had saved his life; the bells didn't really exist; the bells, the bells. They were turning into an urban legend.

Urban legends were Manhattan standards. The circus horse that escaped from Madison Square Garden and swam out to sea with the boy on its back. The coyote that traveled down from the mountains, cutting through backyards in Westchester, to take up residence in Central Park. Alligators in the sewers, of course. Some were real, some too fantastic for words. Danny Byrne's photo of the stone bells, and the miracle of how his life had been spared, fit right in.

The stone bells were about to become a cause célèbre. Sylvester Sr. intuited this and couldn't have been more satisfied. But then his gaze fell again upon the news story, mentioning Daniel and the Rheinbeck Group: *A company spokesman denies any such connection.*

Sighing, the old man looked around his office, at his many diplomas and certificates, his testimonials and photographs. There he was, in black tie, shaking hands with everyone from Henry Kissinger to Hillary Rodham Clinton. Shoulder to shoulder with every New York City mayor—John Lindsay, Abe Beane, Ed Koch, David Dinkins, Rudy Giuliani, Mike Bloomberg.

An entire lifetime of making money and serving the public. Strange, Sylvester Sr. thought as he peered at his wall. There wasn't even one picture of him alone with his son. In groups, yes—gatherings of clients, business associates, government officials. So many mayors.

A knock sounded at the door. Glancing up, Sylvester Sr. saw his son standing in the doorway.

"Good morning," he said, gesturing for him to come in. "Have you seen the papers? Am I right to assume that you're the unnamed 'company spokesman'?"

"Yes," Sylvester Jr. replied. "The *Times* called, and I spoke off the record."

"You denied the boy's involvement with our project," the old man said. His heart constricted. "Even though you know it to be otherwise?"

"I did."

The old man closed his eyes tight. Profit at all costs. Protect the company from scandal, even though the lives of a young man and his family hung in the balance.

"Where is Catherine this morning?" his son asked.

"She left a message on my voicemail. She won't be coming in today." He cleared his throat; somehow he was certain that her absence had to do with Danny Byrne and his family.

"The boy is in a lot of trouble," Sylvester Jr. said. As he gazed across the park toward Belvedere Castle, he looked rather pensive. "Apparently he used a key to enter the castle at will. How he obtained it is unclear. The thinking is that a janitor may have let him use it once, forgotten to get it back. The boy was employed under false pretenses; he tricked the park conservancy into hiring him."

"There are worse things," Sylvester Sr. replied.

"He convinced Catherine to let him use our library. To do *meteorological* research." He spat out the word as if it tasted bad.

"I sometimes think," Sylvester Sr. said, "of how, if I had been a different kind of father, you might have been interested in the park as a place to enjoy. In clouds and the weather station at Belvedere Castle. In the hawks that fly over the city."

"And build nests on balconies, and soil the masonry, and create a general nuisance for co-op boards," Sylvester Jr. said. "Now, Father. Catherine used company funds to pay him for photographs, including the one found in the castle chamber. I'd be remiss if I didn't point out the fact that he knows nothing about photography."

"How difficult is taking pictures?" Sylvester Sr. asked.

"Well, our shareholders will point out that there are professional photographers better suited."

"Aim the camera, snap the photo. Done deal. These pictures were for archival purposes only," the old man said. He felt defeated. He had prayed with his son yesterday. They had faced out the window, asking the Lord for mercy on Daniel Byrne. Yet here Junior was now, focused on the ways their money had been badly spent.

"Yes," his son said. "That is true."

Surprised to find his son in agreement on this point, Sylvester Sr. peered over the tops of his spectacles.

"No one must know that he did photographic work for us," Sylvester Jr. said.

"But—"

"Certainly not the media. If they got hold of that detail, all would be in jeopardy."

The old man lost his temper. He slammed his fist down on his desk, boiling with anger and with utter despair. How could he, a *humanitarian*, have raised such a greedy, selfish, captain of industry?

"All would be lost?" Sylvester Sr. raged. "In what way? Would our stocks lose a quarter point that couldn't be regained in an hour? Would our shareholders be offended by the fact that we hired and attempted to help a young man with a dream?"

"Perhaps," his son said. "But more to the point, they would accuse us of influence peddling."

"Sylvester, have you gone mad? Have I Ebenezer Scrooge as my very own progeny?"

"Father," Sylvester Jr. said quietly, "I've called the city office and made only the merest request. A suggestion, at best. The message will make its way down the channels. Although the investigation will be completed, for the sake of the two minor children, no arrests will be made."

"But . . . what are you saying?"

"Father, our name is worth something in this city. I've called in some favors. This is why I think it's best our involvement be kept quiet. The father will not be arrested. Neither of the children will be, either."

"In the Byrne case?"

His son nodded.

"What made you do this?"

His son's face contorted into a mask of grumpiness. Sylvester Sr. had seen that look on Sylvester Jr.'s face when he was pondering firing someone, or when the stocks hit the skids, or when he didn't like what was being served for lunch. But now, to Sylvester Sr.'s surprise, tears popped into the corners of his son's eyes. They had the effect of softening him, melting away his age. Suddenly the fierce executive standing before him looked like a boy of ten.

"I did it for you."

"Me?" Sylvester Sr. asked.

His son nodded. "All of this started because the boy has a

dream. I know how you feel about dreams, Father. And I knew that you would want the family to have a good Christmas."

Sylvester Sr. felt his own heart expand, almost burst, with joy and gratitude. Staring, he couldn't stop seeing his son as a little boy. They'd called him Chip back then. Chip off the old block.

"Oh, son," he said, welling up.

Sylvester Jr. just stood there, a middle-aged man, starving for his father's approval. Sylvester Sr. saw it in his eyes as he had so many times before—looking up beseechingly, wanting his father to go to a school baseball game, a camp get-together, the planetarium, the hot dog cart—and he felt plagued with ancient guilt.

"I kept thinking of the tree man," Sylvester Jr. said, "wanting to keep his son with him so badly last Christmas. It blinded him to his son's dream. And it made me think, I've been blinded to your dream."

"My dream?"

"Your Look-Up Project," Sylvester Jr. said. "Look up at all the good things. The important things. People have to dream."

"They do," the old man said, his voice ragged. "I've been so worried I failed you. Taught you plenty about the Dow, but nothing about your own heart. Now I see I was wrong. You know."

"It doesn't come naturally," his son said, more humbly than Sylvester Sr. had ever heard him say anything. "But what happened yesterday has got me thinking about it. Merry Christmas, Father."

"Merry Christmas," Sylvester Sr. said, trying to dissolve the lump he had in his throat as he stared at his son, "Chip."

15

*T*he days went by, and Christy sold his trees. People came from all five boroughs and even beyond. They came from New Jersey, Westchester, Long Island, and Connecticut. They paid him top dollar and gave him tips besides. People wanted to have their pictures taken with him. They wanted to ask about Danny. The strangest thing was, he'd lost his silver tongue. He had nothing to say. They'd buy a tree or not—he didn't care. All this attention, wallets just waiting to be emptied, and Christy could only go through the motions.

He was like one of those monks at the abbey up in Cape Breton, people who had taken a vow of silence. As if they'd looked so deeply into their own souls and been struck dumb by the magnitude of what was there. That's how Christy felt. What was there to say? His son's life had been spared, Danny returned to him, if only temporarily. His daughter had stolen their money—rather than ask him to help her brother.

Christy knew that his children did not doubt his love. He didn't doubt theirs. But somehow he had been so focused on his work, and perhaps he had given them the feeling that he had everything under control. Or, as Bridget had said, they just didn't want to bother him. Maybe, just maybe, he'd given them the message that he didn't want to be bothered. Selling his trees, he pondered these possibilities.

Catherine stayed away. Christy watched and waited. While all the rich suburbanites were tying his trees to the tops of their Range Rovers, he'd be looking south, in the direction of her house.

Where was she? All the words Christy wasn't saying to his paying customers seemed to back up, like logs in a river eddy, waiting to spill over to Catherine. He had so many things to ask her, so much he wanted to tell her. But she didn't come.

It took a few days for everything to become untangled: the investigations completed and the paperwork filed. Danny was held for observation at St. Vincent's. Tests were performed, results analyzed. Finally, he was released. He moved back into Mrs. Quinn's, to regain his strength and spend time with his family. In spite of the joy, these were uneasy times.

"Pa, what will happen?" Bridget asked on Christmas Eve. Their trees had just sold out; another year's work was behind them. Now supper was finished, the night drawing to a close. Midnight would be upon them before they knew it, and then it would be Christmas.

Christy glanced across the sitting room at Danny, sitting in a chair, looking through his photographs. They had been returned to him by the police, now that the investigation was over.

"That's up to your brother," Christy said.

"But about *us*," Bridget said. "Are we all in trouble?"

Christy gazed at her. How could he explain to his twelve-year-old that there was trouble—and there was *trouble?* What had possessed her to steal the cashbox? His heart had been aching since he'd seen it fall from the pillowcase.

"Bridget," he said, "you tell me."

Her eyebrows wiggled, and she looked perplexed. "Tell you what?"

"Everything."

"I don't get it."

Danny had been fairly silent himself this last week, about the past year, about his plans for the future. He had kept to himself, sleeping long hours, as if making up for the last three hundred and sixty-five days of life on the streets of New York. But right now Christy could see that he was engaged. He had an unmistakable way of cocking his head as he pretended not to be listening.

"Why don't you tell me," Christy said, "what you want for Christmas?"

"Pa! How can you even ask that? We've had police here left and right! I committed a crime, Pa. I stole all our money. What I want to know is, am I going to jail?"

"You're not going to jail, Bridget."

"And how about Danny, Pa? Is he going?"

"He's not going to jail either."

"You, Pa? Are you going?"

"No. The city's being lenient on me. Even though I've made a total mess of things. Neglected my children."

"Pa, you haven't neglected us," Bridget said.

Christy stared at her. She had Mary's eyes. Green-brown, like soft moss on the north side of a pine trunk. He'd been so busy working hard, trying to raise their kids these last years, he'd hardly had time to miss his wife. But he missed her now. Mary, in her no-nonsense way, would have known how to straighten them all out. She'd been very good at that, placing blame where it belonged. Without her there to point the finger, Christy had to do it himself.

"You're wrong about that, my sweet girl," he said. "I have neglected you terribly. You were so worried, and you didn't tell me. You took matters into your own hands. What signals did I miss, that led you to take the money?"

"I did it for Danny," she said miserably, but gazing at her brother with intense love.

"That's true, and I know it. You had a good motive. But you did a wrong thing."

"We read Robin Hood in school," she said.

"Robin Hood would be on Rikers Island by now, if he lived in New York. I don't want us confusing generosity with crime. Bridget, the child welfare people are telling me you need a therapist."

"Pa, she's not crazy," Danny said.

"It's all my fault," Bridget said, starting to cry. "Acting insane and bringing shame on the family, when all I wanted was to help Danny."

"No one's insane," Christy said, his head spinning and making him feel very crazy himself. "And everyone knows you want to help your brother."

"Are they going to put me in an institution?" Bridget asked.

"Are they going to make me stay here in New York while you go home to Canada?"

"No. They're letting me take you with me. But they want me to find someone for you to talk to. Might be tough in Cape Breton, but we'll manage."

"There might be someone in Ingonish," Danny said.

Christy glanced across the room. Danny seemed so rapt, looking at his pictures. But he kept chiming in—that had to mean something. One of the photos slipped off his lap. Christy glanced down, saw with a pang that it was a stone angel. Catherine's assignment to his son; she had kept him fed this whole year, slipping him money in the only way Danny would have accepted it—employment.

Crossing the room, Christy picked up the picture. He looked at it long and hard. Catherine's spirit seemed to fill the angel's face. He could almost see her clear gray eyes gazing back at him, guiding him in this moment. His heart was pounding as hard as it ever had as he opened his mouth.

"You coming back home with us?" Christy asked. "To help look after your sister?"

Danny shook his head. "Not yet," he said in a voice almost too low to hear.

"What's that?"

"I said 'not yet,'" Danny spoke up louder.

"What are you saying?"

"You asked Bridget what she wanted for Christmas," Danny said, sitting up tall and facing his father. "A few minutes ago. Remember?"

"I remember," Christy said.

"I probably don't deserve anything, but were you going to ask me, too?"

Christy was unprepared for his son's directness. This year on his own had made Danny a man. "I want to know," Christy said, "what you want."

"I want you to trust me, Pa."

Christy frowned. Trust him? He felt himself sliding, right to the edge of a cliff. All Christy wanted was to hold on, grab with all his might, keep everything from falling, falling, into nothingness. He thought of Catherine, of the way he'd felt when he'd found out she'd been helping his son—and he felt himself at the precipice.

"I want to stay here," Danny said. "Not forever—just till I can learn what I need to know."

"Know for what?"

"I want to be a meteorologist. I see what you go through, Pa. Trying to farm the trees, fighting the elements—Pa, it's like you're fighting demons. Wrestling with lightning, hurricanes, drought—you can't stop any of it. But if we knew more about how to predict it, things would be easier for you. You and all the other tree farmers."

"Danny," Christy said, his heart squeezed, as if the hand of God had reached down to take it and rip it right out of his chest, "I want you with me. Me and Bridget. We're a family."

"Pa, don't you think I know that? I know it so much. That's why I have to do this. I'm doing it for you!"

"He is," Bridget said, starting to sob.

"Why couldn't you have told me what you wanted?" Christy asked. "Last year, before all of this happened? Why didn't you talk to me?"

"I didn't want to bother you."

"Bother me?" Christy clenched—thought he'd have a heart attack right then and there. "Am I that terrible, that you can't talk things over with me? Don't you know I love you more than that?"

"You love us so much, you'd kill yourself," Danny said. "You work till after dark. You're out in the field before the sun is up. There's just no time, Pa. No time to talk. I didn't want to worry you with helping me make a decision, when I knew what I was going to do anyway."

"We could have talked, though," Christy said.

"You'd have told me I couldn't do it," Danny said.

And Christy began to cry himself, because he knew it was true. It hurt so much, to love someone as much as he loved Danny— and to watch his path diverge, to see him going in a different direction from Christy and Bridget.

"Didn't you ever have a dream, Pa? Something you knew you had to do?"

Christy thought about that. He'd been too hungry to dream. He'd been too focused on taking over his father's farm, keeping everything going, putting food in his babies' mouths to ever have a dream. And yet . . .

The photo of the angel was right there, between him and Danny. Christy stared down at her, through tears. How crazy his heart felt. If ever he'd had a dream, a desire, this was it. And more than a dream, it could never be. Danny had more chance at learning everything there was to know about the weather than Christy had of being with a woman such as Catherine.

"Pa?"

"Maybe I have a dream now," he said.

"You've got to go for it," Danny said, "if you have one."

"Make it come true," Bridget said.

Christy looked up. His children were staring at him with such intensity, he felt a great shiver go through his bones. Did they know his dream? It wasn't possible. Was he so transparent? He felt himself turn bright red.

"See these pictures?" Danny asked.

"Yes."

"I took them all," Danny said with a strong trace of pride.

"They're very good," Christy said, composing himself. "If this weather thing doesn't work out for you, you can always get a job taking photos."

"Yeah. I was thinking the same thing. Put myself through school, you know? Anyway, I have to make up a list. For the Rheinbecks. About where I took each picture. Mr. Rheinbeck wants to publish a book, hand it out in the schools. Even on street corners, I think. To get all the people in New York to look up."

"And see all the wonders," Bridget said, her eyes shining with love for her brother.

"Right, Bridey," Danny said. "Anyway, I've got the list in my mind. See this angel?" He pointed at the black-and-white photo—the smooth sculpture, the shadows in stone, the wings spread wide, the steady and somehow warm granite gaze.

"Yes," Christy said, staring at the angel and seeing Catherine instead.

"She's a statue by a bridge in Central Park. This one"—he shuffled the pictures, found another angel—"is carved into a church up on Lexington Avenue. And see this gargoyle? It's actually a gryphon, chiseled into the portals of an office building on East Forty-second Street. These demons, or whatever they are," he said, paging through the sheaf of pictures, "are cut into the stone right beside the entrance to Mangia, a restaurant on West Fifty-seventh Street. And these bells . . ."

"The mystery bells!" Bridget said excitedly, quoting a recent *Daily News* headline. The story had focused on the picture of stone bells Penelope had been holding in her hand when Danny took his fall off the roof. She had stayed silent about it, and so had Danny. No one knew where in the city the stone bells were located.

It had become a passionate Christmas scavenger hunt. The city was on fire, questing for the bells. Mr. Rheinbeck himself couldn't be more thrilled—his Look-Up Project was in full swing, even without the final compendium of photos being published. People in all five boroughs were gazing up at buildings, up toward the sky, in search of the stone bells.

Brooklyn residents were convinced the bells were carved into Grace Church, or the Brooklyn Academy of Music, or the great stone footings of the Brooklyn and Williamsburg bridges. One Queens woman claimed that the photo had been taken at a crypt in Flushing Cemetery, right near where her parents were buried.

A young Jesuit was positive the bells were located at Mount Manresa Retreat house, on Staten Island, and Christmas re-treatants found spiritual power in walking the grounds, looking through the house. One wise old priest stood on the hill over-looking the lights of Manhattan, across the water. He knew the exact location of the bells—and it wasn't here. He had seen them when he was a young man growing up in Chelsea.

Minnie Maguire, in the Bronx, walked the whole length of Bainbridge Avenue, positive that if she located the bells, her son Desmond would quit his drinking, take the cure for good.

One couple had found a single bell carved into a granite arch at the Cathedral of St. John the Divine. Moved by the discovery, the man had proposed—a Christmas betrothal inspired by the quest. Right move, wrong bell.

"You going to tell us where they are?" Bridget asked.

"Maybe," Danny said, giving a devilish grin.

Bridget hit him with a pillow. "Come on!"

"I like keeping it a mystery," he said.

"You have to at *least* tell Catherine," Bridget said. "After all she's done for you."

"Yeah," Danny said. "She deserves to know."

Christy waited, watching the look pass between his two children. Danny's grin was catching—Bridget now had it, too.

"She does," Bridget said.

"Pa, you could show her the bells," Danny said.

"I don't know where they are," he said. He saw his son and daughter smiling at him, and he felt himself redden.

"Danny could tell you, Pa," Bridget said.

"I could," Danny said. "If you'd show her where they are, I'll tell you where to find them."

And as Christy listened, Danny did just that.

16

*E*very Christmas Eve, Lizzie and Lucy joined Catherine for a special dinner. They always wore beautiful clothes, including hats, and their best jewelry. They ate oysters, capon, and one truffle wrapped in bacon, grilled in the fireplace embers, and thinly sliced onto the mashed potatoes. For dessert they had *bûche de Noël*. Before Brian's death, they would also place the star on the Christmas tree, open presents, and go to midnight mass at St. Lucy's.

This year there was a new level of festivity. For one thing, Lizzie was very excited about her new boyfriend. During all the time he'd spent patrolling Chelsea, Officer Rip Collins had never seemed to look twice at Lizzie. But this year, because he'd had to stop by

Christy's tree stand so often, he'd finally gotten up the courage to ask her out.

"He took me for a ride in his police car," Lucy said excitedly. "He showed me how to do the perp walk."

"Let's hope that's a skill you'll never need," Lizzie said with a wry look at Catherine.

"Where is he tonight?" Catherine asked.

"On duty," Lizzie said. "Keeping our streets safe for Santa Claus."

"He said he'd bust Santa if he double parks his sleigh," Lucy giggled.

"I think Santa gets special treatment here in Chelsea," Catherine said. "Considering this was where he was made famous. ' 'Twas the night before Christmas,' and all that."

"All that," Lizzie said.

Catherine smiled to see her friend so happy. And she knew that Lizzie felt the same way, guardedly, about her. Something had shifted in Catherine this year. Although she hadn't told Lizzie the details about Brian's visit, Catherine knew that her friend could see that her spirit had lightened.

"It's almost time to go to church," Lucy said, looking at the mantel clock. It was ten-thirty; midnight mass would be crowded, and they wanted to get a seat.

"We should get going," Lizzie agreed. "Are you coming, Catherine?"

Catherine thought. She wanted to. This year so many things had changed. She didn't dread Christmas anymore. She hadn't gotten a tree, so they wouldn't hang the star. And she hadn't bought too many presents, except for some skeins of Icelandic yarn for Lucy, and a silver bracelet for Lizzie. She had thought she would go to midnight mass with her friends this year, but the tight feeling in her chest made her shake her head.

"I need to stay here," she said.

"You could go to see them," Lizzie said, reading her mind.

"The Byrnes?" Lucy asked.

"That's who you're thinking about, isn't it?" Lizzie asked.

Catherine nodded. "They're leaving tomorrow," she said. "I thought they would have come to say good-bye by now."

"I'm going to write to Bridget," Lucy said. "You could write to Christy."

"Helpful, isn't she?" Lizzie asked as she pulled on her coat and walked with Lucy to the front door.

Catherine tried to smile. She'd been keeping the faith ever since that night when she'd locked the attic door. "I just thought he'd have stopped by before now," she said.

"Well, Merry Christmas," Lizzie said, peering out the window.

"What?" Catherine asked.

And then her best friend opened the door. Christy stood on the top step.

"I was afraid it might be too late," he said, looking at his watch. "But I saw your lights on."

"It's not too late," Lizzie said. "Merry Christmas, Christy!"

"Same to you," he said.

"Give our love to Bridget and Harry!" Lizzie said, smiling as she grabbed Lucy's hand and ran down the steps.

Catherine smiled, opening the door wider—to let Christy enter. "Please, come in," she said.

"Actually," he said, holding out his hand, "will you come with me?"

"Right now?" she asked as the wind blew around him, making her shiver.

"Yes," he said. "I have something to show you."

She hesitated, looking into his bright blue eyes. She felt his excitement, and she began to smile. "I'll get my coat," she said.

They got a cab right away, and Christy told the driver to take them to the southeast corner of Central Park. He and Catherine sat in the backseat, not really saying anything, not even daring to look at each other. All those words Christy had wanted to say before escaped him now. He was tongue-tied, lost in a million thoughts. Dreams didn't come with a script. Maybe that's what poets were for, he thought. Poets and songwriters. The cabbie had the radio tuned to a station playing Christmas carols, one after the other.

"What's your favorite?" he asked finally, because he felt so nervous.

"My favorite?"

"Carol," he said. "What's your favorite carol?"

"Hmm," she said. "I'll have to think about that. I like so many. How about yours?"

" 'Silent Night,' " he said. And then he reached into his jacket pocket and removed Danny's photograph of the bells.

"We're going to the park?" she asked finally.

"Yes," he said.

"I thought you'd never want to go back there again," she said, "after what happened to Danny."

"I thought that, too," he said. He thought of what the last few days had brought, all the fear wrought by being caught in the city's bureaucracy, and shuddered. "But some guardian angel must be looking over us. Because Danny's fine. And somehow the authorities have decided we're not criminals."

Catherine smiled, and he couldn't look away. He just wanted to stare at her face, illuminated by all the city lights flashing in the cab windows.

When they got to the corner of Fifth Avenue and Fifty-ninth Street, Christy paid the cabbie, and they all said, "Merry Christmas." Because the street was slippery with snow and ice, Christy took Catherine's hand. He helped her over a snowbank, but she didn't seem to want to let go, even after they walked onto a clear path.

"Do you know where we're going?" he asked as they headed into the park.

"I have an idea," she said, glancing down at the picture he held in his other hand. "Are you going to show me the bells? Is this where Danny took the picture?"

"You'll see," Christy said. They walked under the beautiful iron lamps, throwing orange-yellow light. The pond was frozen, surrounded by snow-glazed bushes. No creatures stirred—it was too cold for birds, animals, and humans alike. Christy felt as if he were walking into a wilderness with her, as if they were alone in the world. Skirting the frozen water, they came to a graceful bridge.

Made of stone, it arched over the narrow northern end of the pond. Still holding hands, they walked to the top of the bridge and looked around. Light from the skyscrapers danced in reflection on the ice. Christy saw Catherine point up at one of the tallest buildings.

"That's my library office up there," she said. "I look down on this bridge every day."

"You do?" he asked, wondering which one was her window.

She nodded. Their breath came out in silvery clouds, and they huddled together, shoulder to shoulder, to stay warm. Her touch made Christy shake inside as he listened.

"Yes. Gapstow Bridge."

"Do you ever look at her?" Christy asked, pointing at a statue hidden in the shadows of the woods just ahead. Although he'd never seen the statue before, he'd known she was right here, from Danny's description and directions.

Catherine peered into the darkness. "An angel," she said, walking down the other side of the curved bridge. From here, Christy could see that it would be obscured by a thicket of trees. "I didn't even know it was here," she said. Looking more carefully at the statue, she touched the folded wings, the wide forehead, the gentle smile.

"She's beautiful," Christy said, staring at Catherine.

"You think it's a woman?" she asked.

Christy nodded. His pulse racing, he put his arms around Catherine, and their eyes met and sparked. He felt calmer, holding her. He wanted her close, this close—there was no other way, he thought. "She's you," he said, pointing at the angel. "From the moment Danny showed me the picture, that's all I could think. She looks just like Catherine."

She shook her head, but he kissed her so she couldn't deny it. How could he be doing this, feeling so afraid of losing this chance, but not wanting one more minute to go by without trying?

Thin clouds blurred the sky. In clear patches, stars blazed as if they were standing on a black Nova Scotia hillside, not here in the middle of Manhattan, surrounded by city light. He gulped cold air, steadying himself. Catherine stared up at him, and

Christy knew life was a scavenger hunt for dreams and that he had finally found his.

"Catherine Tierney," he said, holding her.

"Christy Byrne."

"You're my angel," he said. He hardly dared look around. He was sure the statue would be gone, because he was holding the angel in his arms.

"I was afraid you'd thought I was the opposite"—she smiled—"for being so secretive about Danny."

"You helped him when I couldn't," Christy said. "It took me a while to figure that one out."

Catherine nodded, but she also shivered. A cold wind was blowing through the park, sweeping across the fields and pond, reminding Christy that Christmas Eve was ticking away, and that he still had places to take her.

"Are the bells here?" she asked. "With the stone angel?"

He shook his head, holding her closer to keep her warm. "No," he said. "But I had to bring you here first. So I could show you how I feel. It's not so easy being—the way I am. Words were always what I used to sell my trees. Make a lot of money from all the New Yorkers who walked by. 'Here's a blue spruce, touched with starlight.' Or, 'You won't need tinsel on this Fraser fir—it's got the aurora borealis lighting its branches.' "

Catherine laughed, listening to him sling the sales pitch.

"It's all cheap," he said. "That kind of talk."

"I've heard you say other things," she said.

"Not like what I'm trying to say now," he said. "I don't even have words for what's inside me tonight, Catherine. Nothing that makes any sense, anyway."

She looked up at him, as if she wanted him to try. So he kissed her again, and this time he felt her heart beating as hard as his, right through the fabric of her black coat.

"Danny got right into the spirit of your project," he said. "Taking all those pictures."

"Getting people to look up," Catherine said. "My boss is very grateful to him. The whole city has the fever. Everyone wants to know where he took the picture of those bells."

"Do you want to know?"

"Of course," Catherine said. The city rose up all around them, millions of lives behind the windows of light. It was wild and romantic, and Christy knew that he had joined the throng of people who'd come to New York hoping for a dream to come true.

"Then I'll show you," Christy replied, and he took her hand and led her back across the arch of Gapstow Bridge.

Revelers walked by, on their way back home, or to church, or just because it was Christmas Eve and snow was in the air. Catherine and Christy walked for a few blocks down Fifth, until a cab dropped someone off at the Plaza, and they climbed in.

"Where're you from?" the driver asked, glancing in the rearview mirror. "You from out of town?"

"We're from Chelsea," Christy answered, giving Catherine a smile.

Catherine laughed—his familiarity made her tingle. The driver kept looking. "Hey, you're that tree guy," he said. "Am I right?"

Christy ignored him. Instead he kissed Catherine's neck, cheek, the corner of her mouth. She shivered, leaning into his arms.

"Hey, how's your kid? Is he doing better?"

Silence.

"You're his father, right? The kid who slipped, fell, from the castle? How's he doin'?"

"He's grand," Christy answered. But Catherine could see that the driver had gotten under Christy's skin. She reached for his hand and squeezed it, and he gave her a grateful look. He'd said the angel had reminded him of her; she closed her eyes, thinking of the real angel who had visited New York this week, and she wondered what would happen next.

"You've got to tell me one thing," the driver said.

"Yeah? What's that?" Christy asked.

"You've got to tell me—where are those goddamn bells?"

Catherine smiled, looking out the window. She couldn't believe how excited she felt, because she was about to find out. Like everyone else in New York, she had been captivated by the legend of Danny Byrne, living in Belvedere Castle, possessing not much more than a borrowed camera and a black-and-white photograph of stone bells.

"He must've told you, right?" the driver pressed.

"It's a secret," Christy said. "I wouldn't want to spoil the fun you'll have looking for them yourself."

"Come on. It's Christmas Eve. You're in the business, man. Selling Christmas! All those trees, all that money. How about if I turn up the radio—get you in the Christmas spirit. You've tried that trick, right? I'll do it now, and you'll tell me. How's that?"

"What trick?" Christy asked.

"You know. Turn up the old Christmas carols to get the passersby in the mood. It's what the lights are all about. What all the Christmas windows at all the department stores are all about. It gets people in the spirit to give—to buy. It's what the goddamn tree at Rockefeller Center is all about!"

"That's what I used to think," Christy said.

"Anyway, come on. You're in the giving mood, right? Tell me something no one else in New York knows. You tell me, I'll sell it to the *Post*, and we'll split the proceeds. Talk him into it, lady!"

"I don't think he gets talked into things," Catherine said.

When they'd reached their destination, Tenth Avenue and Twenty-third Street, Christy reached into his pocket and gave the driver a twenty. "Keep the change."

"Hey, it's all about the tips, right?" the driver chuckled. "Better than solving the goddamn mystery of the bells. Thanks, man."

"Merry Christmas," Christy said, and he smiled at Catherine. "Ready?" he asked.

"I am," she said.

The Empire Diner's light flashed, a bright beacon lighting Tenth Avenue. Snow had started to fall. The flakes were fine, veiling the sky. Behind the sheen of snow, apartment lights shone. Catherine shivered, but not from the cold. Christy touched her back, then put his arm around her shoulders. They walked south.

"This used to be farmland," Catherine said as they passed St. Nicholas Park, the postage-stamp-sized square. "Clement Clark Moore owned it all."

"Hard to picture that," Christy said, looking around at all the buildings. Catherine wondered whether he was thinking of his own farm. She wondered what it looked like—how the night sky would look without any city lights, how tall the trees grew, whether he could see the sea from his house.

"You live so far from here," she said.

"I know," he said.

"And you leave to go back home tomorrow."

He didn't reply. Her heart bumped, and they walked along in silence.

"Danny's decided to stay," Christy said slowly. "I don't know exactly what will happen, but Mrs. Quinn has offered to let him have a room in her house if he helps her son John at the hardware store. He seems confident he'll be able to get a scholarship, once he applies to college."

Catherine listened. She was sure that Mr. Rheinbeck—actually, both Mr. Rheinbecks—would want to help Danny however they could. But right now her thoughts were all for someone else's plans.

"What about you, Christy? Do you ever think about staying?"

He held her tighter. They were walking south, and the snow fell harder. It was difficult to see, and the sidewalks were slippery. Catherine's question had sounded almost casual, but just asking it left her feeling shaken. How could he leave? How could he ignore this gift they'd been given? They were holding each other now, walking through the snow. How could they let each other go?

Suddenly Catherine looked ahead and saw St. Lucy's looming before her. People were still streaming in; she checked her watch and saw it was nearly midnight. Her throat tightened—she thought of what had happened inside the church just a week ago. Brian had come back . . . and that was the night that Danny had nearly died.

"Why are we here?" she asked, gazing up at Christy.

His eyes startled her: they were brilliant blue, filled with fire.

Their eyes locked. Catherine shivered, and she reached for his hand. She felt suddenly afraid, as if the world had started spinning faster, faster. The snow drove down from the north, and she huddled closer to Christy.

"Why are we here?" she asked again.

"Don't you know?"

"Lizzie and Lucy are inside," she said. "It's the place I've had all my most important celebrations. It's where I . . ."

"Tell me," Christy urged.

"It's where I said good-bye to the past," Catherine whispered.

"You had to do that," Christy said, sliding his arms around her, pulling her tight, "because this is your future." They kissed again, oblivious to all the churchgoers climbing the stairs behind them. Up in the square tower, the bells began to ring.

"You didn't answer me before," she whispered, as the north wind blew through her hair and made her press closer to Christy. "Do you ever think about staying?"

"I have a farm I have to keep running," he said. "Do you ever think about Nova Scotia?"

"It sounds beautiful," she said, trembling in the snow.

"I'd love to show it to you," he said. "Will you come with us?"

"I want to," she said.

"Then do it."

"I have a job," she began.

"Meeting you was a miracle," he said. "Don't you feel it?"

"I know it," she said, her blood thudding. And she did know. Her heart, shut tight, had been opened by this man and his family. She had followed a ghost, seen angel feathers in the snow, said good-bye to her grief.

"Do you need convincing?" he asked, touching her cheek. "It's okay if you do."

"Convincing?"

"Remember what we came here for," he said.

"Christy, what?" she asked, because in the midst of all the storms, both outside and inside, she'd forgotten. His blue eyes were fierce, gazing at her with such force, she might have been scared. Instead, she felt magnetized.

"Look up," Christy said.

He didn't even have to point. Catherine tilted her head and gasped. There they were: the stone bells.

Sometimes the things that are most familiar are the most foreign. How many times had she walked through this door? She'd been carried into St. Lucy's as a baby, and she'd toddled through as a young child, walked in as a young bride, sleepwalked in as a widow. The bells had been overhead all this time.

"Danny," she said.

"He told me that when you first gave him the camera, he would come down here, to Chelsea, where he had last seen me and Bridget," Christy said. "He said that it made him think of us, feel closer to home. He looked up at this church, and he saw a lot of interesting things to photograph."

"I've walked through this door a thousand times," she said. "I must have seen them before, but I don't remember."

"Your boss is a wise man," Christy said, "to know so much about what people need."

Catherine agreed. She closed her eyes for a moment, feeling the wind blow into her face. There was so much beauty all around, so near at any given moment. "We think we've seen it all before; we think we know it all by heart."

"But we forget," Christy said. "It's so easy to forget."

"Or not to look at all," Catherine said.

"Let's promise each other," he said, his gaze as bright as northern lights. "We won't forget to look."

"I'll remind you," she said. "I promise."

They kissed, and then they looked up again. In the snowy starlight, the church's rose sandstone seemed to glow from within. Blue light streamed through the windows. But it was the stone bells that most caught Catherine's eyes: dusted with snow, coated with ice, they looked silver.

The city lights sparkled down on the street, the sidewalks, the stonework, the silver bells, on Christy Byrne and Catherine Tierney—the tree man from the north country and the librarian from the big city. The snow fell, and the bells of Christmas began to ring.

ABOUT THE AUTHOR

Luanne Rice is the author of *Silver Bells, Beach Girls, Dance with Me, The Perfect Summer, The Secret Hour, True Blue, Safe Harbor, Summer Light, Firefly Beach, Dream Country, Follow the Stars Home*—a Hallmark Hall of Fame feature—*Cloud Nine, Home Fires, Secrets of Paris, Stone Heart, Angels All Over Town, Crazy in Love*, which was made into a TNT Network feature movie, and *Blue Moon*, which was made into a CBS television movie. She lives in New York City and Old Lyme, Connecticut.